"I Can't Date You, Max."

"I can't stop wanting you, Cara."

She lifted her long lashes, her crystal-blue eyes looking directly into his. "Try, Max. Summon up some of your famous fortitude, and try."

He couldn't help but smile at that. "I'm not here for inside information. I was genuinely concerned about you."

"As I said—"

"You're fine. I get it."

That was her story, and she was sticking to it.

Dear Reader,

Welcome to the Harlequin Desire series Daughters of Power: The Capital. I was delighted to be invited to write the opening book. In *A Conflict of Interest,* Cara Cranshaw's loyalties are tested. She is thrilled by the election of President Ted Morrow, but it means an end to her romantic relationship with network journalist Max Gray.

While Max searches for the scandal behind the president's illegitimate daughter, Cara struggles to hide her unexpected pregnancy, since Max has made his opinion on fatherhood crystal clear.

It's always great fun to watch a strong hero discover his softer side. I hope you enjoy *A Conflict of Interest* and all the books to follow in the Daughters of Power: The Capital series.

Happy reading!

Barbara

BARBARA DUNLOP

A CONFLICT OF INTEREST

HARLEQUIN®
entertain, enrich, inspire™

Special thanks and acknowledgment to Barbara Dunlop
for her contribution to the
Daughters of Power: The Capital miniseries.

Recycling programs
for this product may
not exist in your area.

ISBN-13: 978-0-373-73217-3

A CONFLICT OF INTEREST

www.Harlequin.com

Printed in U.S.A.

Books by Barbara Dunlop

Harlequin Desire

Silhouette Desire

*Montana Millionaires: The Ryders
†Colorado Cattle Barons

Other titles by this author available in ebook format.

BARBARA DUNLOP

writes romantic stories while curled up in a log cabin in Canada's far north, where bears outnumber people and it snows six months of the year. Fortunately she has a brawny husband and two teenage children to haul firewood and clear the driveway while she sips cocoa and muses about her upcoming chapters. Barbara loves to hear from readers. You can contact her through her website, www.barbaradunlop.com.

For my husband

* * *

Daughters of Power: The Capital
In a town filled with high-stakes players,
it's these women who really rule.

Don't miss any of the books
in this scandalous new continuity from Harlequin Desire!

A Conflict of Interest by Barbara Dunlop
Bedroom Diplomacy by Michelle Celmer
A Wedding She'll Never Forget by Robyn Grady
No Stranger to Scandal by Rachel Bailey
A Very *Exclusive Engagement* by Andrea Laurence
Affairs of State by Jennifer Lewis

One

It was inauguration night in Washington, D.C., and Cara Cranshaw had to choose between her president and her lover. One strode triumphantly though the arches of the Worthington Hotel ballroom to the uplifting strains of "Hail to the Chief" and the cheers of eight hundred well-wishers. The other stared boldly at her from across the ballroom, a shock of unruly, dark hair curling across his forehead, his bow tie slightly askew and his eyes telegraphing the message that he wanted her naked.

For the moment, it was investigative reporter Max Gray who held her attention. Despite her resolve to turn the page on their relationship, she couldn't tear her gaze from his, nor could she stop her hand from reflexively moving to her abdomen. But Max was off-limits now that Ted Morrow had been sworn in as president.

"Ladies and gentlemen," cried the master of ceremonies above the music and enthusiastic clapping that was spreading like a wave across the hall. "The President of the United

States." His voice rang out from the microphone onstage at the opposite end of the massive, high-ceilinged room.

The cheers grew to a roar. The band's volume increased. And the crowd shifted, separating to form a pathway in front of President Morrow. Cara automatically moved with them, but she still couldn't tear her gaze from Max as he took a few steps backward on the other side of the divide.

She schooled her features, struggling to transmit her resolve. She couldn't let him see the confusion and alarm she'd been feeling since her doctor's visit that afternoon. *Resolve,* she ruthlessly reminded herself, *not hesitation and definitely not fear.*

"He's running late." Sandy Haniford's shout sounded shrill in Cara's ear.

Sandy was a junior staffer in the White House press office, where Cara worked as a public relations specialist. While Cara was moving from ball to ball tonight with the president's entourage, Sandy was stationed here as liaison to the American News Service event.

"Only by a few minutes," Cara shouted back, her eyes still on Max.

Resolve, she repeated to herself. The unexpected pregnancy might have tipped her world on its axis, but it didn't change her job tonight. And it didn't alter her responsibility to the president.

"I was hoping the president would get here a little early," Sandy continued, her voice still raised. "We have a last-minute addition to the speaker lineup."

Cara twisted her head; Sandy's words had instantly broken Max's psychological hold on her. "Come again?"

"Another speaker."

"You can't do that."

"It's done," said Sandy.

"Well, *un*do it."

The speakers, especially those at the events hosted by organizations less than friendly to the president, had been vetted weeks in advance. American News Service was no friend of President Morrow, but the cable network's ball was a tradition, so he'd had no choice but to show up.

It was a tightly scripted appearance, with only thirty minutes in the Worthington ballroom. He would arrive at ten forty-five—well, ten fifty-two as it turned out—then he was to leave at eleven-fifteen. The Military Inaugural Ball was next on the schedule, and the president had made it clear he wanted to be on time to greet the troops.

"What do you want me to do?" asked Sandy. "Should I tackle the guy when he steps up to the microphone?" Sarcasm came through her raised voice.

"You should have solved the problem before it came to that." Cara lifted her phone to contact her boss, White House Press Secretary Lynn Larson.

"Don't you think I tried?"

"Obviously not hard enough. How could you give them permission to add a new speaker?"

"They didn't *ask*," Sandy pointed out with a frown. "Graham Boyle himself put Mitch Davis on the agenda for a toast. Two minutes, they say, tops."

Mitch Davis was a star reporter for ANS. Graham Boyle might be the billionaire owner of the network, and the sponsor of this ball, but even he didn't get to dictate to the president.

Cara couldn't help an errant glance at Max. As the most popular investigative reporter at ANS's rival, National Cable News, he was a mover and shaker himself. He might have some insight into what was up. But Cara couldn't ask him about this or anything else to do with her job, not now and not ever again.

Cara pressed a speed-dial button for her boss.

It rang but then went to voice mail.

She hung up and tried again.

She could see that the president had arrived at the head table, in front of and below the stage. He was accepting the congratulations of the smartly dressed guests. The men wore Savile

Row tuxedos, while the woman were draped in designer fabrics that shimmered under the refracted light of several dozen crystal chandeliers.

The MC, popular ANS talk show host David Batten, returned to the microphone. He offered a brief but hearty welcome and congratulations to the president before handing the microphone over to Graham Boyle. According to the schedule, Graham had three minutes to speak. Then the president would have one dance with the female chair of a local hospital charity and a second with Shelley Michaels, another popular ANS celebrity. That was to be followed by seven minutes at his table with ANS board members before taking his leave.

Cara gave up on her cell phone and started making her way toward the stage. There was a staircase at either end, nothing up the middle. So she knew she had a fifty-fifty chance of stopping Mitch Davis before he made it to the microphone. Too bad she wasn't a little larger, a little brawnier, maybe a little more male.

Once again, her thoughts turned to Max. The man dodged bullets in war-torn cities, scaled mountains to reach rebel camps and fought his way through crocodiles and hippos for stories on the struggles of indigenous people. If Max Gray didn't want a person up onstage, that person was not getting up onstage. Too bad she couldn't enlist his help and would have to rely on her own wits.

She chose the stairs at stage right, wending her way through the packed crowd.

Graham Boyle was waxing poetic about ANS's role in the presidential election. He'd taken a couple of jabs at President Morrow's alma mater and its unfortunate choice of mascot given current relations with Brazil. But that was all fair game.

Cara wished she was taller. At five foot five, she couldn't see the stairs to know if Mitch was waiting to go up on the right-hand side. She regretted having gone for the comfortable two-inch heels instead of the flashy four-inch spikes that her sister, Gillian, had given her for Christmas. She could have used the height.

"Where are you going?" It was Max's voice in her ear.

"None of your business," she retorted, attempting to speed up and put some distance between them.

"You have that determined look in your eyes."

"Go away."

He tucked in close beside her. "Maybe I can help."

"Not *now,* Max." She was working. Why did he have to do this to her?

"Your destination can't possibly be a state secret."

She relented. "I'm trying to get to the stage. Okay? Are you happy?"

"Follow me." He stepped in front of her.

His six foot-two-inch height and broad shoulders made him an imposing figure. She supposed it didn't hurt any that he was famous, either. Last month, he'd been voted one of the ten hottest men in D.C. The upshot was he could move through a crowd far faster than she could. Resigned, she stuck to his coattails.

Even with Max clearing the way, they eventually got stuck behind a crowd of people.

"Why do you want to get to the stage?" He turned to ask her.

"For the record," she responded, "I don't know any state secrets. I don't have that kind of job."

"And since I'm not a foreign spy, we should be able to carry on a conversation without compromising national security."

An unmistakable voice came over the sound system. "Good evening, Mr. President," drawled Mitch Davis.

A murmur of surprise moved across the room, since Mitch was a known detractor of President Morrow. Cara rocked back on her heels. She'd failed to stop him.

"First, let me say, on behalf of American News Service, congratulations, sir, on your election as President of the United States."

The applause came up on cue, though perhaps not as strong as usual.

"Your friends," Mitch continued with a hearty game-show-host smile, "your supporters and your mother and father must all be very proud."

Cara strained to catch the president's expression, wondering if he would be angry or merely annoyed by the deviation from the program. But there was no way to see through the dense crowd.

"The president is smiling," Max offered, obviously guessing her concern. "It looks a little strained though."

"Davis is not on the program," Cara ground out.

"No kidding," Max returned, as if only an idiot would think otherwise.

She glared at him, then elbowed her way past, maneuvering through the crowd toward the president's table below the stage. Lynn Larson was going to be furious. It wasn't exactly Cara's responsibility to ensure that this specific ball went smoothly, but she had been working closely with the staffers coordinating each one. She was partly to blame for this.

Thankfully, Max didn't follow her.

"I expect nobody is prouder than your daughter," said Mitch, just as Cara reached a place where she could see Mitch on stage.

There was a confused silence in the room, because the president was single and didn't have any children. Confused herself, Cara rocked to a halt a few feet from Lynn at the president's table. Lynn glanced toward the stairs at the end of the stage, as if she was gauging how long it would take her to get there.

Mitch waited a beat, microphone in one hand, glass of champagne in the other. "Your long-lost daughter, Ariella Winthrop, who is with us here tonight to celebrate."

It took half a second for the crowd to react. Maybe they were trying to figure out if it was a sick joke. Cara certainly was. But she quickly realized it was something far more sinister than a joke, and her gaze flew to the corner of the stage, where she'd glimpsed her friend Ariella, whose event-planning company had been hired to throw the ANS ball. When Cara focused on Ariella, her stomach sank like a stone. As soon as it was pointed out, the resemblance between Ariella and the president was quite striking. And Cara had known for years that Ariella was adopted. Ariella didn't know her birth parents.

The crowd's murmurs rose in volume, everyone asking each other what they knew, had heard, had thought or had speculated. Cara could only imagine at least a thousand text messages had gone out already.

She took a half step toward Ariella, but the woman turned on her heel, disappearing behind the stage. There were at least a dozen doorways back there, most cordoned off from the guests by security. Hopefully, Ariella would make a quick getaway.

Mitch raised his glass. "To the president."

Everyone ignored him.

Cara moved toward Lynn as the crowd's questions turned to shouts and the press descended on the table.

"If you would direct your questions to me," Lynn called, standing up from her chair and drawing, at least for a moment, the attention of the reporters away from President Morrow.

The man looked shell-shocked.

"We obviously take any accusation of this nature very seriously," Lynn began. She looked to Cara, subtly jerking her head toward the stage.

Cara reacted immediately, skirting around the impromptu press conference to get to the microphone onstage. Damage Control 101—get ahead of the story.

She quickly noted that the security detail had surrounded the president, moving him toward the nearest exit. She knew the drill. The limos would be waiting at the curb before the president even got out the door.

She had no idea if the accusation was true or if Mitch Davis had simply exploited the resemblance between Ariella and the president. But it didn't matter. The texts, tweets and blogs had likely made it to California and Seattle, probably all the way across the Atlantic by now.

Cara scooted up the stairs and crossed the stage, staring Mitch Davis down as she went for the microphone.

He relinquished it. His work was obviously completed.

Mitch's gaze darted to the crowd. His confident expression faltered, and she saw Max, his eyes thunderous as he moved along below the stage, keeping pace with Mitch as the man made his way to the stairs.

"Ladies and gentlemen," Cara began, composing a speech inside her head on the fly. "The White House would like to thank you all for joining the president tonight to celebrate. The president appreciates your support and invites you all to enjoy yourselves for the rest of the party. For members of the press, we'll provide a statement and follow-up on your questions at tomorrow's regular briefing."

Cara turned to applaud the band. "For now, the Sea Shoals have a lot of great songs left to play tonight." She gave a signal to the bandleader, which he thankfully picked up on, and the energetic strains of a jazz tune filled the room.

Covered by the music, Cara quickly slipped from the stage.

Max was standing at the bottom of the stairs to meet her, but her warning glare kept him back—which was probably the first time that had ever happened. But then he mouthed the word "later," and she knew they weren't done.

There were times when being a recognizable television personality was frustrating and inconvenient. But for Max Gray, tonight wasn't one of them. He'd only been to Cara's Logan Circle apartment a handful of times, but the doorman remembered him from his national news show, *After Dark,* and let him straight into the elevator without calling upstairs for Cara's permission.

That was very convenient for Max, because there was a better than even chance Cara would have refused to let him come up. And he needed to see her.

The ANS inaugural ball debacle had been a huge blow to the White House, particularly to the press office. Cara and Lynn had handled it professionally, but even Cara had to be rattled. And she had to be worried about what happened next. The scandal whipping its way through D.C. tonight had the potential to derail the White House agenda for months to come. Max needed to see for himself that Cara was all right.

He exited the aging elevator into a small, short hallway. Her apartment building had once been an urban school, but it now housed a dozen loft apartments, characterized by high ceilings, large windows and wide-open spaces. Cara's had a small foyer hall off the public hallway. From there, a winding staircase led to a light-filled, loft-style grand room with bright walls and gleaming hardwood floors. The single room had a marble-countered kitchen area in one corner, with a sleeping area separated by freestanding latticework wood screens.

Max had loved it at first sight. It reminded him of Cara herself, unpretentious, breezy and fun. She was practical, yet unselfconsciously beautiful, from her short, wispy, sandy-brown hair to her intense blue eyes, from her full, kissable lips to her compact, healthy body. She never seemed to run out of energy, and life didn't faze her in the least.

The short public hallway had four suite doors. The last time Max had been here was mid-December. Cara had kept him at arm's length after Ted Morrow won the election in November. But he'd bought her a present while he was in Australia, pink diamond earrings from the Argyle Mine. He'd selected the raw stones himself, them had them cut and set in eighteen-karat gold, especially for her.

She'd let him in that night, and they'd made love for what was likely the last time—at least the last time during this administration. Cara had been adamant that they keep their distance, since he was a television news host, and she was on the president's staff. Max shuddered at the thought. He really didn't want to wait four years to hold her in his arms again.

He knocked on Cara's door, then waited as her footsteps sounded on the spiral wrought-iron staircase.

He heard her stop in front of the door and knew she was looking through the peephole. There were a limited number of people who could get through the lobby without the doorman announcing them. So she probably expected it was Max. That she'd come down the stairs at all was a good sign.

"Go away," she called through the door.

"That seems unlikely," he responded, touching his fist to the door panel.

"I have nothing to say to you."

He moved closer to the door to keep from having to raise his voice and alert her neighbors. "Are you okay, Cara?"

"Just peachy."

"I need to talk to you."

She didn't respond.

"Do you really want me to talk from out here?" he challenged.

"I really want you to leave."

"Not until I make sure you're okay."

"I'm over twenty-one, Max. I can take care of myself."

"I know that."

"So, why are you here?"

"Open up, and I'll tell you."

"Nice try."

"Five minutes," he pledged.

She didn't answer.

"Ten if I have to do it from the hallway."

A few seconds later he heard the locks slide open. The door yawned to reveal Cara wearing a baggy, gray T-shirt and a pair of black yoga pants. Her feet were bare, her hair was slightly mussed and her face was free of makeup, showing the few light freckles that made her that much cuter.

"Hey," he said softly, resisting an urge to reach out and touch her.

"I'm really doing fine," she told him, lips compressed, jaw tight, her knuckles straining where she held the door.

He nodded as he moved inside, easing the door from her hands to close it behind himself. He looked meaningfully at the spiral staircase.

"Five minutes," she repeated.

"I can finish a soft drink in less than five minutes."

She shook her head in disgust but headed up the stairs anyway. Max followed, resisting once again the urge to reach out and touch. There was a time, a very short time in the scheme of things, when he'd felt free to do that.

"Cola or beer?" she asked, coming to the top of the stairs and padding across the smooth floor to the kitchen area.

"Beer," Max decided, shrugging out of his tux jacket and releasing his bow tie.

He moved to the furniture grouping of two low, hunter-green leather couches, a pair of matching armchairs and low tables with lamps, all tastefully accented by a rust, gold and brown patterned rug. Her view of the city was expansive. The night had turned clear, with a new blanket of snow freshening up the buildings and the trees, reflecting the lights in the park across the street.

Cara returned with a can of beer for him and a cola for her. She handed the can to Max and then curled into one of the armchairs, popping the top on her own drink.

"Four minutes," she warned him.

He opened his beer and eased onto the corner of a couch. He pulled off his wristwatch and set it on the coffee table, faceup where he could see it.

He caught her slight, involuntary smile at the gesture.

"You okay?" he asked in a soft voice.

"I'm fine," she assured him one more time.

"Did you know?" he couldn't stop himself from asking.

"You know I can't answer that."

"Yeah," he agreed. "I was counting on being able to read your expression when you told me to back off."

She lifted her brows. "And did you?"

"You're as inscrutable as ever."

"Thank you. It helps in my business." She took a sip.

He followed suit. Then he set the can down on a coaster. "You know I'll have to go after the story."

"I know you will."

"I don't want to hurt you. And I respect the hell out of this president. But a secret daughter?"

"We don't know for sure she's his daughter."

Max stilled. He was surprised Cara had offered even that much insight. "We will soon enough."

She nodded.

"Have you talked to Ariella?" He knew the two women were friends. Cara had casually introduced Max to Ariella at a fundraising event right before the election.

Cara set her cola down on a table beside her. "Do you honestly think that would be in anyone's best interest?"

"That's neither a yes nor a no."

Cara's expression remained completely neutral.

"You're very good," he allowed.

She sat forward. "I know you have to go after this, Max. But can you at least be fair about it? Can you please take into account all the facts before you help ramp up the public hysteria?"

Max leaned forward, bringing them close enough that he could feel her faint breath, inhale the coconut scent of her shampoo, close enough that it was hard to keep from kissing her.

"I always take all the facts into account."

"You know what I mean."

He reached for her hand.

But at his faintest touch, she snapped it away. "This is going to get ugly."

He knew that was an understatement. The press, not to mention the opposition, smelled blood in the water, and they were already circling. "Are you going back to work tonight?"

"Lynn's taking the night shift. I'll go in early tomorrow morning."

"It's going to be a long haul," Max noted, wishing there was something he could do to help her. But he had a very different job from Cara, a job that was certain to be at odds with hers.

"Yes, it is." She sounded tired already.

"I'll be fair, Cara."

"Thank you." There was a wistful note to her voice. For a moment, her blue eyes went soft and her expression became less guarded.

He reached for her hand again, this time squeezing before she had a chance to pull away.

She glanced at their joined hands. Her voice turned to a strained whisper. "You know all the reasons."

"I disagree with them."

"I can't date you, Max."

"I can't stop wanting you, Cara."

She lifted her long lashes, and her crystal-blue eyes looked directly into his. "Try, Max. Summon up some of your famous fortitude and try."

He couldn't help but smile at that. "I'm not here for inside information. I was genuinely concerned about you."

"As I said—"

"You're fine. I get it."

That was her story, and she was sticking to it.

Her skin was creamy and smooth, her lips dark, soft and slightly parted. He imagined their feel, her taste, her scent, and instinct took over. He tipped his head, leaning in.

But she pulled abruptly away, turning and dipping her head before he could kiss her. "Your five minutes are up."

He heaved a sigh, giving up, letting her small hand slip from between his fingers. "Yeah. I guess they are."

* * *

Max had left his watch behind in Cara's apartment. She had no way to know if he'd done it on purpose. It was a Rolex—platinum, with baguette-cut emeralds on the face. She couldn't even imagine the price. Being a popular television personality definitely had its perks.

When she'd gone to bed, Cara had set the watch on the table beside her. She'd used its alarm as a backup, since she'd had to get up at three-thirty.

Then she'd put it in her purse before heading for her West Wing office at the White House. If Max called about it, she'd drop it off for him on her way home. She had no intention of letting him use it as an excuse to come back to her apartment again.

She flashed her ID tag through the scanner in the White House lobby, and passed through security in the predawn hours. A cleaner was vacuuming, while deliverymen made their way along the main hall. It was quiet out front, but closer to the press office, the activity level increased. Movers were lugging furniture and boxes into the newly appointed offices. She passed several people on her way to her small office.

"Morning, Cara." Her boss, Lynn, fell into step with her.

Cara unbuttoned her coat and unwrapped her plaid scarf from around her neck as they walked. "Did you get a chance to talk to the president?"

Lynn shook her head, shifting a file folder to her opposite hand. "The Secret Service was with him for an hour. Then Barry went in for a while. And after that, he went back to the residence."

"Is it true?"

One of the communications assistants appeared to take Cara's scarf and purse. Cara shrugged out of her coat and added it to the pile in the woman's arms.

"We don't know," said Lynn, pushing open her office door.

Cara followed her inside. "Barry didn't ask him?"

Chief of Staff Barry Westmore knew the president better than anyone.

As press secretary, Lynn's office was the largest in the communications section. It housed a wide oak desk, a long credenza, a cream-colored couch and three television screens mounted along one wall playing news shows from three different continents. In English, German and Russian, reporters were speculating on the president's personal life.

Lynn plopped down in her high-backed leather chair, twisting her large, topaz ring around and around the finger of her right hand. Lights from the garden broke the darkness outside the window before her. "Even if it's true, the president wasn't aware that he had a daughter."

"That's good." From a communications perspective, deniability was key in this situation.

Lynn didn't look as relieved as Cara felt. "There's more than one possible woman."

Cara's eyebrows shot up.

"Barry and I did the math," said Lynn. "Accounting for possible variations in gestation period. Since the baby might have been premature, there are three possible mothers."

"Three?" Despite the gravity of the situation, Cara found herself fighting a smile. "Go, Mr. President."

Lynn frowned at her impertinence. "It was senior year in high school. The man was a football star."

"Sorry," Cara quickly put in, lowering herself into one of the guest chairs opposite the desk.

Her boss waved away the apology. "He's refusing to give us the names."

"He has to give us the names."

"First, he wants to know if Ariella is his daughter. If and only if she is his daughter, then we can look at the ex-girlfriends."

"The press will find them first," Cara warned, her mind flitting to Max. The networks and newspapers would pull out all the stops to find Ariella's mother. They wouldn't wait on a DNA test. This was the story of the century.

"Yes, they will," Lynn agreed. "But the president is unwilling to ruin innocent lives."

In Cara's opinion, the women's lives were already ruined. Anyone who'd had the misfortune to sleep with President Morrow in high school would be fair game. It wouldn't even matter whether the lovemaking squared up with Ariella's birth date; they'd still be hunted down and hounded with questions.

Lynn twisted her ring again. "It's always that thing that you don't see coming. And it's always sex. Next time, remind me to back a nerdy candidate. Maybe president of the chess club or something."

"These days, nerds are hot," Cara pointed out.

"That's because we expect them to grow up rich."

"That's why I hang out at the local internet café looking for dates."

Lynn grinned, putting a little life into her exhausted expression. "I should have married a nerd in high school."

"Instead of a smoking-hot navy captain?"

Lynn gave a self-conscious shrug, but her eyes took on a secretive glow. "It was spring break. And he rocked those dress whites."

"You didn't even look twice at the nerds," Cara accused.

"The hormones want what the hormones want."

Cara's brain conjured up a picture of Max, but she quickly shook it away. "Have you spoken to Ariella?"

"Nobody can find her."

"Can't blame her for that." If it had been Cara, she'd have crossed the Canadian border by now.

"Think you can find her?" Lynn asked.

Cara would love nothing better than to find Ariella and make sure she was okay. But she wasn't going to abandon Lynn to go on a wild-goose chase. "You need me here."

"We can live without you."

"Just what every woman wants to hear. You're going to have to give a statement to the press today. And you need me to write it. *You* need to get some sleep."

Cara wished she'd had more than three hours' sleep herself. She knew she had to pay more attention to things like eating and sleeping now that she was pregnant. But time for sleep and time to prepare nutritious meals were pretty hard to come by while working for the president. Especially during this crisis.

"I will get some sleep," Lynn agreed. "Barry's working on a statement, and we'll put the press off until the afternoon. Do you think you'd be able to find Ariella?"

Cara got to her feet. She had to believe her womb was a safe place for the first few weeks of gestation no matter what chaos was going on outside it. She reassured herself that many women wouldn't even know they were pregnant this early.

"I can try," she told her boss.

"Then go. Get out of here."

Cara headed for her own office, quickly retrieving her coat and purse. If she could find Ariella, at the very least they could offer her Secret Service protection. She wrapped the scarf around her neck before heading out into the snow.

If the story was true, Ariella would need protection for the rest of her life, and that would only be the start of the chaos. Merely being a member of the White House staff had sent Cara's personal life into a tailspin. She couldn't imagine what Ariella was going through.

Two

After combing the city for countless hours, looking everywhere she could think to find Ariella, Cara gave up. It was nearly nine in the evening, and she'd left dozens of messages and asked everyone who might know anything. She was exhausted when she finally took the elevator back to her loft. Maybe Ariella really had fled to Canada.

Cara twisted her key in the dead bolt, then unlocked the knob below, pushing open the solid oak door.

As soon as she stepped inside, she knew something was wrong. A light was on upstairs and someone was playing music.

Her hand reflexively went to her purse, where she'd stashed Max's watch. If he'd used it as an excuse to come back, if the superintendent had actually let him into her apartment, well, there was going to be hell to pay for both of them. Max might be a famous television personality, trusted and admired by most of D.C., but that didn't give him the right to con the super, break into her apartment and make himself at home.

She tossed her coat and scarf on the corner bench in the

entry hall and pulled off her boots, not even bothering to put them in the closet. She paced her way up the spiral staircase, working up her outrage, planning to hit him with both barrels before he had a chance to start the smooth talk.

Then she realized Beyoncé was playing. And it smelled like someone was baking. She made it to the top of the stairs and stopped dead.

Ariella stood in the middle of her kitchen, surrounded by flour-sprinkled chaos. She had one of Cara's T-shirts pulled over her short dress and a pair of red calico oven mitts on her hands. Midstep between the oven and the island counter, she held a pan of chocolate cupcakes.

"I hope you don't mind." She blinked her big, blue eyes. "I didn't know where else to go."

"Of *course* I don't mind." Cara quickly made her way across the room. "I've been out looking for you."

Ariella set down the cupcake pan. "They've staked out my house, the club, even Bombay Main's. I didn't dare go to a hotel, and I was afraid of the airport. The doorman always remembered me, and I pretended I misplaced your spare key."

"You were right to come here." Cara gave her a half hug, avoiding the worst of the flour.

Then she glanced at the trays of beautifully decorated cupcakes. Vanilla, chocolate and red velvet, they were covered in mounds of buttercream icing, and Ariella had turned marzipan into everything from flowers and berries to rainbows and butterflies.

"Hungry?" she jokingly asked Ariella.

"Nervous energy."

"Maybe we can take them to the office or sell them for charity." There had to be five dozen already. They couldn't let them go to waste.

Ariella pulled off the oven mitts and turned off the music. "You got any wine?"

"Absolutely." Cara's wine rack was small, but she kept it well stocked.

She moved to the bay window alcove to check out the selection. "Merlot? Shiraz? Cab Sauv? I've got a nice Mondavi Private Selection."

"We might not want to waste a good bottle tonight."

Cara laughed and pulled it out anyway.

"I'm going for volume," said Ariella.

"Understandable." Cara returned to the kitchen, finding a small space among the mess to pull the cork. "Glasses are above the stove," she told Ariella.

Ariella retrieved them, and the two women moved to the living room.

Ariella peeled off the T-shirt, revealing a simple, steel-gray cocktail dress. She plunked into an armchair and curled her feet beneath her. "Do we have to let it breathe?"

"In an emergency—" Cara began to pour "—not necessary."

Ariella rocked forward and snagged the first glass.

Cara filled her own and sat back on the couch. Then she suddenly remembered the pregnancy and guiltily set the glass down beside her. What was she *thinking?*

"Mine can breathe for a few minutes," she explained. Then focused on Ariella. "How are you holding up?"

"How would you guess I'm holding up?"

"I'd be flipping out."

"I am flipping out."

"Could it be true?" Cara asked. "Do you know anything at all about your biological parents?"

Ariella shook her head. "Not a single thing." Then she laughed a little self-consciously. "They were Caucasian. I think they were American. One of them might have grown up to be president."

"I always knew you had terrific genes."

Ariella came to her feet, moving to a mirror that hung at

the top of the stairs, gazing at her reflection. "Do you think I look anything like him?"

Cara did. "Little bit," she said, rising to follow Ariella and stand behind her. "Okay, quite a bit."

"Enough that…"

"Yes," Cara whispered, squeezing Ariella's shoulders.

Ariella closed her eyes for a long second. "I need to get away, somewhere where this isn't such a big deal."

"You should stay in D.C. We can protect you. The Secret Service—"

"No," Ariella's eyes popped wide.

"They'll take good care of you. They know what they're doing."

"I'm sure they do. But I need to get out of D.C. for a while."

"I understand." Cara wanted to be both sympathetic and supportive. Ariella was first and foremost her friend. "This is a lot for you to take in."

"You are the master of understatement."

Their eyes met in the mirror.

"You need to take a DNA test," said Cara.

But Ariella shook her brunette head.

"Not knowing is not an option," Cara gently pointed out.

"Not yet," said Ariella. "It's one thing to suspect, but it's another to know for sure. You know?"

Cara thought she understood. "Let us help you. Come to the office with me and talk to Lynn."

"I need time, Cara."

"You need help, Ari."

Ariella turned. "I need a few days. A few days on my own before I face the media circus, okay?"

Cara hesitated. She didn't know how she was going to go back to her boss and say she'd found Ariella and then lost her again. But her loyalty was also to her friend. "Okay," she finally agreed.

"I'll take the DNA test, but not yet. I don't think I could wrap my mind around it if it was positive."

"Where will you go?"

"I can't tell you that. You have to keep a straight face when you tell them you don't know."

"I can lie."

"No, you can't. Not to the American press, you can't. And not to your boss, and definitely not to your president."

Cara knew she had a point. "How can I contact you?"

"I'll contact you."

"Ariella."

"It has to be this way."

"No, it doesn't. We can help you, protect you, find out the truth for you."

"It has to be this way for me, Cara. Just for now. Only for a while. I know it's better for the president if I stay, better for you if I stay and face the music." Her voice broke ever so softly. "But I just can't."

"None of this is your fault," Cara felt compelled to point out, putting an arm around Ariella's shoulders.

Ariella nodded her understanding.

"He's a very good man."

"I'm sure he is. But he's the president. And that means…" Ariella's voice trailed off.

"Yeah," Cara agreed into the silence. That meant the circus would never end.

Her cell phone chimed a distinctive tone, telling Cara it was a text from Lynn. She moved away and pulled it from her pocket. The message told her to turn on ANS.

"What?" asked Ariella, watching Cara's expression.

"It's from Lynn. There's something going on. It's on the news." Cara moved to the living area and pressed a button on the remote, changing the channel to ANS.

Ariella moved up beside her. "Oh, I have a bad feeling about this."

Field reporter Angelica Pierce was speaking. She was speculating about Ariella and her relationship to the president, and
was saying something about a woman named Eleanor Albert
from the president's hometown of Fields, Montana. Then old
yearbook photos of the president and Eleanor Albert came up
side by side on the screen. With a dramatic musical flourish,
a picture of Ariella settled in between them.

Cara's eyes went wide.

Ariella sucked in a breath, gripping the sofa for support.
"No," she rasped.

Cara wrapped her arm around her friend and held on tight.
There was no mistaking the resemblance. Cara wasn't even
sure they needed a DNA test.

Max knew the excuse of having forgotten his watch in
Cara's apartment was lame. But it was the best he'd been able
to come up with on short notice. She was home now. He could
see the lights on in her apartment.

He'd just seen the pictures of the president, Ariella and Eleanor on a news site on his tablet. All hell was about to break
loose at the White House, and it was doubtful he'd be able to
see Cara again for weeks to come.

He exited from his Mustang GT, turning up his coat collar
against the blowing snow. He was on his way home from dinner with the NCN network brass and wearing dress shoes, so
he was forced to dodge puddles, taking a circuitous route on
his way across the street.

He made it to the awning, brushed the flakes from his
sleeves, then looked up, straight into the eyes of Ariella Winthrop. They both froze.

"Ariella?" He swiftly glanced both ways to see if anyone
else was out on the dark street.

"Hi, Max."

He moved close, taking her arm to guide her away from
the streetlight. "What are you doing? You can't be out on the

street." There didn't appear to be any other reporters around, but it wasn't safe for her. He'd met her only a few times, but he liked her a lot. She was Cara's close friend, and Max seemed to have a protective streak when it came to Cara.

"The doorman called me a cab."

"A cab? Have you seen the news? You're plastered all over it."

"I saw."

"Let me take you home." He immediately realized that was a ridiculous suggestion. "Let me take you to a hotel. I'll take you anywhere you need to go. But you can't stand out here alone waiting for a cab."

He made a move toward his own car, but she stood her ground, tugging her arm from his.

"Max," she commanded.

He reluctantly stopped and turned to her.

"You're one of the guys I'm avoiding, remember?"

"I'm not a reporter right now."

"You're always a reporter."

"You don't have to talk. Don't say a word." He paused. "But can I ask you one question?"

She shot him an impatient look.

He asked anyway. "Was it you? Did you leak tonight's information to ANS?"

"I'd never even heard of Eleanor Albert before tonight. And the pictures don't prove a thing. I still don't know for sure."

He recognized that she was in denial. "The rest of the world knows for sure," he told her gently. "Let me take you to the White House."

"No!"

"You'll be safe there." And maybe it would earn him some goodwill with the administration, maybe even with Cara.

Wait a minute. Cara. Why was Cara letting Ariella leave her apartment all alone? Why hadn't she called in reinforcements?

"Did you talk to Cara up there?" It occurred to him that maybe Cara wasn't home.

"That's two questions," said Ariella.

"Is she upstairs? She let you leave?"

"I'm a grown woman, Max."

"And you're the president's daughter."

"Not until they prove it, I'm not."

A new thought occurred to Max. And, if he was right, it wasn't a half bad idea. "Are you going into hiding?"

Her silence confirmed his suspicions.

"I can help. I can take you somewhere safe."

This time she rolled her eyes. "It won't be hiding if an NCN reporter knows where I am. You're already going to report this entire conversation."

Max was used to walking fine ethical lines. He couldn't lie to his network, but he could choose the facts he shared and the order in which he disclosed them. "It's up to me to decide how to frame my story."

Her expression was blatantly suspicious. "What does that mean?"

"What do you want me to report?"

She hesitated, then seemed to decide she had little to lose. "That I have no knowledge of my biological parents, and I've left the D.C. area."

"Done."

"You'd do that for me?"

"Yes," he told her with sincerity.

But her guard was obviously still up. "Are you serious?"

"I am serious."

After a moment, her expression softened. "Thank you, Max."

"At least let me take you to Potomac Airfield. You'll be able to grab a private charter and take it anywhere you want to go. If you need money—"

"I don't need money."

"If you need anything, Ariella."

"How can you take me to Potomac and not report on it?"

He put on his best broadcaster voice. "Sources close to Ariella Winthrop disclose that she has left the D.C. area, likely on a private plane out of Potomac. Nothing is known about the destination, the aircraft or the pilot."

He gave another glance around the dark street to make sure they were still alone. "You can put up your hair, Ariella. We'll stop somewhere and buy you a pair of blue jeans, a baseball cap and dark glasses. Take a Learjet or something even better. Those guys don't talk about their passengers."

He could feel her hesitation. Her teeth came down on her lower lip.

"You got a better idea?" he asked.

"What's in it for you?"

"Goodwill. Yours, eventually the White House's and the president's. Plus, I'm a nice guy."

"You're with the press."

"I'm still a nice guy. And I'm a sucker for a maiden in distress."

That brought a reluctant smile to her lips.

"My car's across the street." He nodded to the Mustang. "Every minute we stand out here, we risk someone recognizing you."

Just then, a taxi pulled up and stopped at the curb, its light on.

Ariella glanced at it. But then she nodded to Max. "Take me to Potomac Airfield."

"Two things," Lynn said to Cara from behind her office desk.

It was ten the next morning, and Lynn had just finished addressing reporters in the press room for a second day in a row. So far, President Morrow had remained out of sight, his schedule restricted to small, private functions where the White

House could control the guest list. But Cara knew that was about to change. He was scheduled to attend a performance tonight at the Kennedy Center.

"Eleanor Albert is an obvious priority." Lynn counted her points off on her fingers. "Who is she? *Where* is she? Is she really Ariella's mother? And what will she say publicly about the president? Two, there's a whole town full of people out in Fields, Montana. We need to know what they know, what they remember and what *they're* going to say publicly."

Then she glanced up, her attention going to someone in the doorway behind Cara.

"There you are," she said, waving her hand for the person to enter. "You might as well come on in."

Cara turned, starting in astonishment as she came face-to-face with Max. He was dressed in blue jeans and square-toed boots, with an open-collar white shirt beneath his dark blazer. He was freshly shaved. His perpetually tousled hair, wide shoulders and rugged looks gave him a mantle of raw power, even though he was just a visitor to the West Wing.

He met her gaze, his expression neutral.

Even with Lynn in the room, Cara had a hard time controlling her annoyance. Max had gone on national television last night, disclosing what he knew about Ariella's whereabouts. She didn't know who his source had been, but he'd milked it for all it was worth, tossing both Ariella and the White House to the wolves in his quest for ratings.

"Have a seat." Lynn pointed to the chair next to Cara's. The two chairs were matching brown leather, low backed but rounded and comfortable, with carved mahogany arms.

Max moved guardedly, but he did as Lynn asked.

"Who's your source?" Lynn shot out without preamble.

"Seriously?" asked Max with an arch of one brow, a carefully placed thread of amazement in his tone.

"How did you learn about Ariella?"

Cara was curious as well. Even she hadn't known Ariella

was headed for Potomac Airfield. She couldn't imagine who had found out, or why they would tell Max of all people.

"You know perfectly well that I can't disclose my sources," Max said to Lynn, but he cast a glance Cara's way, as well.

"You can when it's a matter of security," Lynn countered. "This might even be national security."

Max sat back in his chair, "Really? Go on."

"If she's kidnapped," said Lynn, twisting her ring. "If a foreign entity, or heaven help us all, a terrorist, gets their hands on the president's daughter, it will absolutely be a situation of national security."

"You don't know that she's his daughter."

"Do you think the terrorists care? I was convinced by those pictures. And I'm pretty sure the rest of the nation was convinced by them, too. Do you think the president will take the chance that's she's not?"

Max's body became alert. "So, you're saying the president slept with Eleanor Albert."

Lynn's face paled a shade. "I'm saying nothing of the kind."

But Max pounced on her small misstep. "If he hadn't slept with her, this couldn't possibly be a matter of national security."

For a moment, Lynn was speechless.

Cara stepped in. "Who told you Ariella was going to Potomac Airfield?"

Max twisted his head to look at her. His eyes were cool, his expression a perfect, professional mask.

Cara pressed him. "Come on, Max. You don't want Ariella hurt any more than we do. She's innocent in all this. She needs Secret Service protection."

"No kidding," said Max. "And did you tell her that last night?"

Cara blinked, her insides clenching up.

He continued, "Did you tell her she needed the Secret Service?"

There was only one way for him to have known Ariella had

come to Cara. "Of course I did. I begged her to let me help. I just finished explaining that to Lynn."

Max turned back to Lynn. "You want to know my source? Ariella is my source. I know she went to Potomac Airfield because I drove her there. She's gone, Lynn."

Lynn sat up in her chair. "Why on earth didn't you stop her?"

"Because the power of the press doesn't extend to kidnapping and forcible confinement. She's a grown woman. She's an American citizen. And she's free to come and go as she pleases."

"Is she still in the country?" Cara asked.

"She told me she had her passport."

"You didn't report on any of that last night."

He slowly turned back to Cara, his expression reproachful. "I didn't, did I?"

"You want points for that?" Cara demanded.

"It would be nice. A little credit. A little consideration. Maybe a scoop or two. I ran into Ariella. I offered her assistance. And I put her safety and the good of my country ahead of my own interests. She was determined to leave D.C. without notice. I thought it was best to give her a fighting chance at successfully doing that."

Cara found herself nodding in agreement with his words. She knew from personal experience that there'd been no talking Ariella out of her plans. She only hoped she came back soon. A DNA test was in everyone's best interest.

Lynn's demeanor changed. "The White House appreciates your efforts," she told Max.

"I would imagine you do." He came to his feet. "I'm not the bad guy here. But I do have a job to do."

As he left the office, Lynn's phone rang. Cara quickly took the opportunity to jump up and go after him.

"Max?" She hurried down the hall.

He stopped and turned back, and she canted her head toward her own office.

He followed her inside, and she closed the door. Sure, he'd done the right thing. But he wasn't completely off the hook.

"Where did you run into Ariella?" she fired off.

"Logan Circle."

"My apartment."

"Yes."

"You stalked her."

He moved toward Cara, making her heart reflexively race and her breath go shallow. It didn't seem to matter how hard she fought or how much logic she sent through her brain, over and over again. She was compulsively attracted to Max Gray. It seemed to be embedded in her DNA.

"Really?" he demanded. The distance between them was far too small. "That's what you think? That I was staking out your apartment on the off chance that Ariella would come by?"

Cara admitted the mathematical odds had been low on that happening. She took a step back, bumping against the edge of her desk.

His eyes glittered meaningfully as he moved again, keeping the distance static. "You can't think of any other reason? None at all?"

"I told you no, Max."

"I was there for my watch."

"We both know that was a ruse."

"Yeah. We do. But you won't let me play it straight, Cara. I have no other choice."

"Your choice is to stay away."

"That's not working for me."

There was a shout in the hallway and the sound of two sets of footsteps going swiftly past.

"We can't do this here," she told him.

"When and where?"

"Never and nowhere."

"Wrong answer."

"It's the only answer you're going to get. I have to go to work, Max. In case you missed it in the papers, we're having a crisis."

His tone went suddenly soft. "I'm sorry for that. I truly am."

"But you have a job to do, too," she finished for him.

"And I better get to it."

He brushed the backs of his knuckles against hers, sending a spike of awareness ricocheting through her system, squeezing her heart and tightening her abdomen.

Before she could protest, he'd turned and was gone.

Cara made her way around her desk, dropping into her chair. She gave a reflexive glance at her computer screen, knowing that a million things needed her attention, but the email subject lines didn't compute inside her brain.

Her hand dropped to her stomach and rested there. She was barely pregnant. If not for her ultraregular cycle and modern, supersensitive home pregnancy tests, she wouldn't even know it yet.

But she did. And she was. And Max's baby was complicating an already dicey situation. Max was one of the ten hottest men in D.C. She didn't need a magazine to tell her that. He was also smart, funny, innovative and daring.

He wanted her. That much was clear. But what he didn't want, what he'd never wanted and never would want, was home, hearth and family. He'd told her about his single mother, how his father walked out on them, how he was no genetic prize and had no plans to carry on his questionable family legacy.

He'd found his niche in broadcasting. He had an incredible instinct for a story, and he was absolutely fearless about going after it. It didn't matter if it was in Africa or Afghanistan, flying high in the air or on the bottom of the ocean. He'd chase a story down, and once he caught it, he'd bring it home and broadcast it to the awe and attention of millions of Americans. Max had everything he'd ever wanted in life.

She'd tried to stay away from him from the very start. Given their careers, a relationship was risky during the campaign, foolish after the vote count and impossible now that the president had taken office.

On more than one occasion, it had occurred to Cara that Max might want her for the sole reason that he couldn't have her. And sometimes, in the dead of night, Cara fantasized about giving in to him, spending as much time as she wanted in his company, in his bed. She wondered how many days or weeks it would take for him to tire of her. She also wondered how fast and far he'd run if he knew the extent of her feelings for him.

For Max, this was just another lark, another fling, another woman in the long line that formed a part of his adventurer, bachelor lifestyle. But for her, it was different. She'd all but given him her heart. And now she was having his baby.

If he'd run fast and hard from the knowledge of her true feelings, he'd rocket away from the possibility of fatherhood. He'd be on the next plane to Borneo or Outer Mongolia.

Cara gave a sad smile and coughed out a short laugh at her musings. In the dead of night, when she fantasized about Max, it was those initial few days and weeks that occupied her thoughts. She glossed over the part where he left and broke her heart. Some days, she actually thought it might be worth it.

Three

The things Max put up with for his job. He'd hacked his way through jungles, gone over waterfalls, battled snakes and scorpions, even wrestled a crocodile one time. But nothing had prepared him for this. He was slope side in the president's hometown of Fields, Montana, among five hundred darting, shrieking schoolchildren let loose on skis and snowboards.

While the president was growing up, Fields had been a small town, mostly supported by the surrounding cattle ranches. But over the years, its scenic mountain location and pristine slopes had been discovered by skiers and snowboarders. Lifts had been built and high-end resort chains had moved in, fundamentally changing the face of the entire town.

Ranch access roads still lined the highway, but the old-guard cowboys now rubbed shoulders with the colorfully attired recreation crowd. It seemed to Max a cordial if cautious relationship. While the newer parts of town were pure tourism, the outskirts were a patchwork of the old and new. A funky techno bar had been built next to the feed store, while a tavern with sawdust and peanut shells covering the floor shared a parking lot with a high-end snowboard shop.

Max's cameraman, Jake Dobson, sent up a rooster tail of snow as he angled his snowboard to a halt next to Max. The two men had first worked together at a small, local station in Maryland. When Max had been asked to join the team at NCN, he'd made it clear that Jake coming with him was a condition of the contract. Jake was the unsung hero in every single one of Max's news stories.

"Another run?" asked Jake.

"I don't think so," Max scoffed, glancing at the multitude of children on the slope. "I was scared to death out there."

Jake laughed at him. "They're quite harmless."

"I'm not worried about them hurting me. But it's like dodging moving pylons. Pylons that bruise easily. I'm not about to have running over an eight-year-old girl on my conscience."

"We could do a black diamond run."

They had a couple of hours left before dark.

"Sure. Up there, I can take out a twelve-year-old. That'll help me sleep better." Max bent down to pop the clips on his own snowboard.

"It's a statewide outdoors club jamboree," Jake put in helpfully as he released his own bindings. "They'll be here for a week."

"We've got work to do anyway." Max stood his board up in the snow, removing his helmet and goggles.

The two men had spent the morning in the older part of Fields, talking to the ranching crowd. So far, they'd met a number of people who'd known the president when he was a teenager. Unfortunately, none of them were willing to go on camera. And none would admit to knowing anything about Eleanor.

"I think the ranchers have all headed home by now," Jake observed. "Early to bed and early to rise."

"Maybe. But their kids and grandkids will be at clubs dancing with the tourists. Who knows what kind of stories have been passed down about the Morrows?"

"You're going to play the tourist and mix and mingle?"

"Why not?" Max had been pleasantly surprised by how respectful the people of Fields seemed to be. It was obvious many of them recognized him from his television show, but they mostly smiled and nodded and kept their distance. Few even asked for autographs.

Back in D.C.—and in New York and L.A.—people were much more aggressive. It was impossible for him to walk into any restaurant, lounge or club in D.C. without being approached by a dozen people. Being in Fields was quite refreshing.

"Can we get a burger first?" Jake asked, brushing the snow off his board with the back of his glove. "I'm starving."

"Works for me." Max started to walk back to the lodge. "Are those pip-squeaks really going to be here all week?"

His and Jake's rooms were uncomfortably close to the indoor pool complex. There'd been a steady stream of shrieking and stomping children up and down their hall both last night and this morning.

"Yes, they are," Jake responded. "I talked to one of their leaders up top."

"Lovely," Max drawled.

He wasn't a kid person. Some people seemed to see right past the noise, the mess, the smell and the irrationality to the cute, lovable little tykes beneath.

Max was in awe of those people. He preferred rationality. Or, at least, predicable irrationality. If there was one thing he'd learned about adults, it was they could always be counted on to act in their own best interests.

"I called down and asked the hotel manager to move us," said Jake.

Max brightened. "You did?"

"I've got your back, buddy." Jake smacked him on the shoulder. "We're each in a one-bedroom villa up on the hillside. It's adults only."

"I love you, man."

Jake chuckled. "It was the hot spring pools that made up my mind. Well, that and the fact that Jessica walked out on me last week. I don't want to spend my first assignment as a bachelor surrounded by grade-schoolers."

"Jessica walked out on you?"

Jake pulled off a glove with his teeth. "She'll be back. But until then, I am under no obligation to be faithful to her."

"She's clear on that?"

They took the staircase leading to the equipment lockers.

"I'm single and she's single. She can bang half of D.C. while I'm gone for all I care."

"I take it she's not 'the one.'"

"It's way too soon to tell."

Max couldn't help but grin at that as they entered the cavernous, warehouselike building. "Trust me, Jake. If she was the one, you'd kill any guy who looked sideways at her, never mind slept with her."

"You're an expert?" Jake scoffed.

"I know that much."

Max wasn't even Cara's boyfriend and he had a hard time thinking about her with any other guy. Technically, the two of them were single. But that was only a technicality, based on current circumstances. It didn't mean he'd look twice at another woman.

They stowed their boards and gear, changed out of the snowboard boots and headed for the Alpine Grill on the street out front. Max was still pondering his and Cara's single status when the waitress brought them each a mug of red ale from a local microbrewery.

He and Jake had taken seats on the lounge side of the rustic, hewn-beam restaurant, which was adults only. But the shrieks and cries of children came through the doorway from the restaurant. Then a group of people burst into a rollicking rendition of "Happy Birthday." Evidently, someone named Amy had reached a milestone.

"Shall I mention that it's your birthday?" asked Jake.

"Now that would be a treat," Max returned dryly.

He took a drink of the foamy beer. He'd turned thirty today. Some people thought of it as a milestone. Max didn't see it that way. He'd been twenty-nine and three hundred and sixty-four days yesterday. Thirty was only twenty-four hours older. He really didn't get the big deal.

Jake craned his neck. "Good grief, they gave those little kids sparklers."

Max turned to look.

When he did, it wasn't the potential fire hazard that caught his eye. It was Cara. She was standing in the restaurant foyer, looking adorable in a waist-length, puffy, turquoise jacket, a pair of snug blue jeans and set of ankle-high black books. Her cheeks were bright red, her lips were shiny and her blue eyes were as striking as ever.

Max's chest went tight. He scraped back his chair and rose from the table.

"Nobody's on fire," Jake pointed out. "Yet."

Max didn't respond. His attention was locked on Cara as he instinctively wound his way through the other tables. The shrieks of the children, the smell of grilling beef, the rainbow of ski clothing disappeared from his perception.

"Hello, Cara." He offered her a friendly smile.

In response, her eyes went round with obvious shock and her jaw dropped open a notch. "Max," she managed. "You're in Fields."

"I'm in Fields," he returned.

She gave her head a little shake, as if she was trying to wake herself from a dream. But Max wasn't going anywhere.

The hostess appeared in front of them. "For two?" the young woman asked, glancing from Cara to Max.

"Just one," said Cara.

"Join us," said Max. "Jake is here," he quickly finished, so she wouldn't think it would look like a date.

Cara had met Jake a couple of times over the past few months. As far as Jake was concerned, Cara was an acquaintance of Max's, no different than hundreds of other people on the periphery of his life as a news reporter.

Cara hesitated while the woman waited, her bright, welcoming smile flickering with confusion.

Cara glanced to Jake, then obviously concluded refusing his offer would garner more curiosity than accepting it would.

"Sure," she said to Max. "Why not?"

Max thanked the hostess, then guided Cara to their table.

When they got there, Max introduced her. "You remember Cara Cranshaw."

Jake got to his feet. His smile was warm and his eyes alight as he shook Cara's hand. "It's *very* nice to see you again."

Max instantly realized his mistake. Jake and Cara were both single. Sure, Jake was in the news business like Max. But a cameraman was quite a few steps removed from the people who actually researched and crafted the stories. He'd be a much safer choice for Cara.

And Jake certainly seemed to appeal to women. He was tall, physically fit, square-chinned and gray-eyed, with a devil-may-care attitude that got him a steady string of offers from women all around the world.

"Cara doesn't date newsmen," Max announced.

Cara shot him an appalled expression.

But Jake laughed easily. "I'm sure she can make an exception in this case."

This time she blanched, gripping the back of her chair. And Max realized she'd drawn the conclusion Jake knew about their relationship.

"Jake means for him," Max pointed out.

"What do you say?" Jake asked her easily. "My girlfriend just dumped me. I'm wounded and terribly lonely."

Cara seemed to recover from her shock very quickly. She smoothly took her seat and unfolded the burgundy cloth napkin in front of her.

Then she looked to Jake. "I'm afraid I don't go on pity dates."

Jake clutched at his chest as if he'd been stabbed.

"Better for you to stay away from the ones with brains, anyway," Max said to Jake.

"Aren't you cynical," Cara chided Max.

"Because I don't think Jake can get a date with a woman whose IQ is over one hundred?"

"Because you seem to think there's a critical mass of low-intelligence women for him to choose from."

"Ouch," said Jake.

"I didn't mean to offend your gender," said Max.

"Which makes it that much worse," she said tartly.

"Keep digging, buddy," said Jake, making shoveling motions with his hands. To Cara, he said. "Can I get you a drink?"

Max cursed himself for being slow on the uptake.

"Thank you," Cara responded with a sweet smile for Jake. "Ginger ale, please."

Jake glanced around the crowded pub, obviously checking for their waitress. After a moment, he rose to walk over to the bar himself.

"He's a gentleman," said Cara, her tone a rebuke to Max as she smoothed the napkin out in her lap.

"He's flirting with you."

She rolled her eyes. "Really, Max. Thank you for clearing that up, since, like many women, I'm of low intelligence and wouldn't have figured it out for myself."

Max clamped his jaw, fighting the urge to defend himself. Instead, their gazes locked, and an instant rush of desire washed through him as the noise of the crowd ebbed and flowed.

Cara cracked first. "So, what are you doing in Fields?"

"Same thing as you."

"I doubt that."

"We're both here after the story."

She straightened in her chair. "No. You're here after the story. I'm here looking for the truth."

"Don't get all self-righteous on me. It's not an attractive quality."

She leaned in and hissed, "You think I want to be attractive? To you?"

He lowered his voice, matching her posture. "There's no way for you to help it, sweetheart."

Jake's arrival broke the moment. "Your ginger ale, ma'am."

Cara turned to him and smiled. "Thank you, sir."

"Pleasure to be of assistance."

Max snagged his beer mug by the handle, struggling not to gag on the syrupy sweetness. "Give me a break."

"Did you know it was Max's birthday?" Jake asked Cara in a hearty, if slightly malicious, voice.

"I did not." She gave Max an overly sweet smile. "Happy birthday."

"I think we should get the staff to sing."

Max glared his annoyance at Jake. "I think the fistfight that would break out between us afterward would reflect badly on NCN."

Jake laughed easily, leaning back in his chair.

Just then, the "Happy Birthday" chorus came up again in the restaurant. This time it was Billy being celebrated.

Before the voices died down, a little girl shrieked and cried. Probably Billy's little sister, jealous because he was getting all the attention. She sounded very young, and Max could only hope they didn't appease her by handing her a lit sparkler.

"Kid heaven," he muttered under his breath. "Adult hell."

Cara shot him an odd look. But then her cell phone rang and she dug into her purse to retrieve it.

"Sorry," she apologized to them both before raising the phone to her ear. "Hi, Lynn."

Cara ran her finger up and down against the condensation of her ginger ale glass, distracting Max while she listened.

"Uh-huh," she finally answered. "Will do. Tomorrow?" She went silent. "Got it. Thanks." She hung up and slipped the phone back into her purse.

"Care to share?" Max asked.

She gave him a secretive smile that tightened his stomach. "You wish," she teased.

"I think she's one up on us," Jake joked.

That wasn't news to Max. Cara had been one up on him from the first moment they'd met.

Later that day, Cara had started her search with the school yearbook. It was easy enough to find the president's and Eleanor Albert's classmates. The ones she'd tracked down so far didn't remember enough to help the press with the story. That was encouraging. As long as they continued to say they didn't know anything, and as long as Eleanor didn't surface, there wasn't much more to report.

Despite the encouraging news, by the end of the first day, Cara returned to her hotel room exhausted. She was worried about running into Max again, and she knew there would be other reporters in town, so she decided on room service.

She found herself adding a glass of milk to the order, making sure she had both green and yellow vegetables and a good balance of protein and complex carbs. She'd have loved to go for the chocolate cake for dessert, but settled instead for frozen yogurt with strawberries.

She'd also added a multivitamin to her diet, and booked an appointment with an obstetrician for later in the month. She wasn't ready to pick up any baby books yet, but she did browse a few sites on the internet. She found she could think about diet and exercise and body changes without panicking, but if she let her mind go to an actual baby, she'd find herself dizzy and short of breath.

Like now. When an ad came up for infant formula and a cherubic little baby smiled out from her phone, she quickly shut down the browser, closing her eyes until the feeling passed. She knew she had to wrap her head around this. To do that, she needed someone to confide in, and there was only one person in the world who fit the bill.

She pressed a speed dial button on her cell phone.

After a few rings, her sister Gillian's voice came on. "Hey, Cara."

Cara forced a cheerful tone. "Hey, yourself."

"How are things in D.C.?"

"Hectic. Seattle?"

"Right back at you. We're opening up a sales office in Beijing next month. You would not believe the red tape." Gillian's voice went muffled for a moment. Then she came back to the call. "Sorry about that."

"Are you still at work?"

"It's only seven on this side of the country. You home?"

"Are you…" Cara hesitated. "I mean, I know you're always busy, but…is it worse now than normal?"

"Not particularly. Hey, Sam, tell them I'll sign it off, but only if it's under a million… Sorry again."

Cara couldn't help but smile at Gillian's familiar pace of life. Her sister was CEO of her own technology company. They'd broken into the health-care market with GPS organizational devices that tracked everything from room cleaning to medication dispensing three years ago and never looked back.

"No problem," said Cara. "I'm the one who's sorry to bother you."

"It's no bother. So, what's going on?"

Cara didn't know how to answer that.

Gillian jumped back in. "I mean, I read about the secret daughter and all. I assume that's taking up most of your time."

"It is."

"Did he know? I mean… Okay, this isn't a secure line, and even if it was…" Gillian took a breath, speaking by rote. "I know you wouldn't give away confidential information about the president to your sister. So, all you FBI guys listening in can stand down."

Cara laughed. She appreciated her sister's caution, but it wasn't necessary. The FBI wasn't listening in on her phone calls.

Gillian's voice went warm again. "So, what do you need, baby sister?"

Though they were only fourteen months apart, Gillian had teased Cara with the term most of their lives.

"Any chance you could take a trip to Montana?"

"Montana? Why in the heck would I go to Montana?"

"Fields, Montana."

"Ooohhh," Gillian drawled. "*That* Montana. Back where the whole thing started. Why? You need me to sleuth something out? Bribe someone?"

"You know, if the FBI really was listening, you would end my career in a single phone call."

"Did I say bribe?" Gillian came back. "I meant *find*. You want me to *find* someone?"

"I want you to come and see me."

There was a split-second pause. "You're in Montana."

"Yes."

"Right now?"

"Right now."

"That's less than an hour away. I can have the jet ready by eight."

Cara allowed herself to hope. "Can you come?"

"Is something wrong?"

"No." Cara scratched at a flaw in the hotel desktop. "No, no. Nothing much."

Again Gillian hesitated almost imperceptibly. "But it's something. Is it work?"

"Nothing to do with work. What you see on the news is pretty much it right now. There's the Asia Pacific Summit coming up in L.A., but beyond that it's all Ariella all the time. Is she or isn't she, and when did the president know."

"So, it's personal?"

"Can you come?"

"Are you sick?"

"No."

"Did you break the law?"

"Gillian."

"Do you need money? Do you have a secret gambling addiction? Is the mob after you?"

"No."

"Because, I've got a lot of capital tied up in Beijing right now, but I'm sure I could free up—"

"I don't need your money."

"Okay. So, what's going on? Are you pregnant?"

Cara froze. She knew she should toss out something flippant to throw Gillian off the truth, but she couldn't for the life of her think of what that might be.

"Cara?"

"Please. Just come."

"I'm on my way."

Cara was the last person Max expected to see walking into the small Fields airport this late at night. Despite its small size, it was an attractive airport, themed around the frontier spirit of the region, with lots of polished pine logs, leather and field-stone. But it had also been designed and built with the high-end ski clientele in mind, so it was tasteful and welcoming.

Right now, it was all but deserted. The concourse shops

and cafés were closed. The waiting areas were empty. Most of the staff still on site were cleaners, with the exception of a lone clerk behind the check-in counter. Max moved from the alcove where he'd sat down, crossing the floor toward Cara.

Hearing his footsteps, she turned.

As she had in the Alpine Grill, she looked startled and none too pleased.

"You *are* stalking me," she charged, glancing around, probably checking for Jake and his camera.

"I was about to accuse you of the same thing." He came to a halt beside her.

"I'm here to meet someone," she told him

"There are no flights this time of night."

"It's a private jet."

"Uh-huh." He watched her expression, trying to guess her intentions. If she'd simply been following him on spec, then she didn't know who he was meeting. On the other hand, if she somehow found out who he was meeting, she might have followed him here because of it.

She remained inscrutable. "And you?"

"Meeting someone myself." He'd give her that much.

"Who?" she fired back.

He shook his head. "Uh-uh."

She crossed her arms over her chest. "I don't believe you."

He widened his stance. "Believe whatever you want."

"You promised you wouldn't take advantage of our relationship."

"What relationship?" If they were having a relationship, Max would dearly love to know.

"You know what I mean. You can't…" She glanced around. "It's not fair…." She seemed to force herself to gather her thoughts. "Can't you just leave? This is nothing. I promise you, this is nothing."

"Do I have to remind you this is a public airport and a free country?"

She had him curious now. If she hadn't followed him here, there was a chance she was hiding something herself. Maybe he'd stumbled across something important.

"Cara!" a woman called from across the concourse.

Cara immediately left Max's side, rushing to meet the woman who had emerged from an airside doorway.

The two met in the middle of the room. The woman dropped her overnight bag, and they hugged. It was then Max realized how much they looked alike. Their hairstyles were similar, same wispy, short look. The light brown hair color was nearly identical, and their eyes, noses and mouths were almost copies. The other woman was slightly taller, and Cara was a little leaner.

Max automatically started toward them.

"Max Gray." He stuck out his hand to the other woman.

"Really?" the woman singsonged, glancing at Cara as she disentangled from the embrace. "Then you must be—"

"He's a reporter," Cara blurted out. "And we have to be *very* careful what we say around him." Her warning to the woman was surprisingly blunt.

"I host an investigative news show," Max corrected her. "It's called *After Dark* on NCN." He wasn't particularly snobbish about the difference, but he didn't want the woman to think he was some lowlife tabloid stringer, either.

"I'm Gillian Cranshaw. Cara's sister."

"There's certainly a family resemblance."

"We have to go now." Cara hooked her arm through Gillian's, scooped up the overnight bag and all but dragged her sister in the direction of the exit.

"Let me." Max stepped forward, reaching for the bag.

"I've got it," said Cara, quickening her pace. Something obviously had her rattled.

"Catch you later," Gillian called back over her shoulder.

Before Max could give much thought to Cara's bizarre behavior, a man appeared through the same airside doorway as

Gillian. Cara glanced fleetingly at him but otherwise paid no attention.

Clearly, there was some kind of family drama on top of the political drama. Otherwise, Cara might have taken a moment to wonder who exactly Max was meeting at almost ten o'clock at the Fields airport. And it was worth wondering about. But Max certainly wasn't going to do her job for her.

"Liam Fisher?" Max asked as the man approached.

"Hello, Max. I recognize you from your program."

"Thank you for coming."

"Thanks to NCN for thinking of me."

The two men shook hands.

Since arriving in Fields, Max had learned two things. One, the town was intensely loyal to the president. And two, Eleanor Albert hadn't ever made much of an impression. Few people remembered her, and even fewer people associated her with Ted Morrow.

Combined, those two details told Max one very important thing. The story of Eleanor's daughter Ariella had been hard to get. And conventional means likely hadn't been enough to dig it out in the first place. That meant unconventional, possibly illegal, means had been used to obtain the scoop.

Liam Fisher was a former staffer at ANS. He'd left under a cloud of secrecy and at odds with the current owner, Graham Boyle. Max's instincts were telling him that the real story wasn't Eleanor Albert. The real story was ANS and how they'd found out about Eleanor Albert in the first place.

Four

Cara hustled her sister around a small airport café, past a candy store and behind the security kiosk toward the side door that led to the parking lot.

"For a minute there, I thought he was the daddy," said Gillian as they briskly walked toward the exit. She twisted her head for a final look at Max, then did a quick check of her cell phone.

"He's a reporter," Cara responded, not about to get into an explanation right now. "And I think he's following me."

"I think he's meeting the guy who came in on the Cessna," said Gillian. "They were landing behind us."

"Reinforcements," Cara guessed. "The place is crawling with press."

"I read about it. You know that Ariella person, don't you? Isn't she the caterer who did that Thanksgiving thing? The one where the singer fell into the cake."

"That's her," Cara acknowledged.

They made their way down a concrete ramp to the mostly deserted parking lot where Cara had left her rented SUV.

"She seems like she has a good sense of humor," Gillian observed.

"So does the president."

"So, you think it's true then?"

"What do you mean?"

"You just compared Ariella's sense of humor to the president's. You must think she's his daughter. Or do you *know* she's his daughter?"

"I don't know anything for sure." Cara hit the unlock button on the remote and got a double beep in response. "But you must have seen the pictures on TV."

"Nope."

"Well, Ariella looks an awful lot like them. I mean, not only does she look like Eleanor Albert. She looks like the president, too. A perfect combination of genes." Cara opened the hatchback door and tossed her sister's bag inside.

"Then that's that. It must be true."

"If I had to bet," said Cara. "My money would definitely be on yes."

"But they'll do DNA."

"They will."

"Surely the president can put a rush on it."

Cara headed for the driver's door. "You really don't watch much TV, do you?"

Gillian's cell phone rang. "I've been mostly paying attention to tech sector news coming out of China and India." She raised the phone to her ear. "Hello?" Using her free hand, she opened the passenger door and climbed into the vehicle.

Cara followed suit, buckling up and starting the engine. Then while Gillian talked business on her phone, Cara backed out of the parking spot and headed for the parking lot exit.

Judging from Gillian's side of the conversation, it sounded as though there was trouble with a supplier in India. Then Gillian took another call and had an argument with her accountant about staff pension plans. By the time she hung up, they were nearly back to town.

"It would have been a genetic jackpot," she announced, tucking the phone back into her slacks pocket.

"For Ariella?" Cara glanced from the snowy road to her sister, then quickly back again.

"No. That Max guy, the reporter. Tall, good-looking, seemed athletic. And you have to be a quick thinker to host a news show. So he must have a brain up there."

Cara wasn't so sure about Max's reasoning skills. "He does a lot of dangerous fieldwork. Jungles, war zones, mountaintops."

"So brave, too?"

"I meant that his testosterone seems to be crowding out his intellect. You want to stop for a drink?" On impulse, Cara wheeled into the Pine Tree Lounge parking lot. It was a newer log building on the outskirts of Fields, with inviting yellow lights on a pine-pillared porch.

"Sure," Gillian agreed. "I'm up for liquor."

They locked the vehicle and made their way along the shoveled walkway, up a wide, stone staircase and into a wood-paneled entry. A country tune played softly through the speakers, and the polished wood tables were lit with tiny oil lamps. The chairs were red leather, and vintage horse tack adorned the walls.

Cara moved to a quiet table near the back, checking to be sure they were out of earshot of the other patrons.

The waitress arrived immediately, setting down glasses of ice water. Gillian gave a cursory look at the extensive wine list, then simply asked for something "really good" in an old-world cabernet sauvignon.

Finally, they were alone. Cara wasn't driving, and Gillian's cell phone wasn't ringing.

"So," said Gillian with a deep breath as she reached for the bowl of mixed nuts in the middle of the table.

"So," Cara returned, bracing herself. "It's him. He's the guy."

Gillian glanced both ways, looking over her shoulder.

"What guy?"

"Max. He's the father."

Gillian's hand dropped to the tabletop. "Then why—"

"He doesn't know. He can't know. We're not supposed… He's a reporter, and I work in the White House press office."

"But you slept with him anyway?"

"That was before the election." Cara defended herself. "And, okay, once after the vote count, but it was all before the inauguration. And that was a mistake. It never should have happened."

"Whoops," Gillian deadpanned.

"That's pretty much what I said. And he… And I… And then…" Cara waved her hand in the air. "You know what I mean."

Gillian fought a smile. "I'd know what you meant if you finished your sentences, or at least finished your clauses."

Cara dropped her chin to her chest and shook her head. "I mean, I'm screwed."

Gillian waited until Cara looked up. Her eyes were glowing with what looked like joy. "You are not screwed. You're going to have a baby. *We* are going to have a baby." She reached for Cara's hand. "You don't have to worry about a thing. It doesn't matter how this happened. It's great that it did. Babies are never bad news. Especially yours."

"He doesn't want children," said Cara. "He's never wanted children. He wants to chase stories to dangerous places around the world and not have to worry about anyone back home."

"Bully for him."

"And even if he did," Cara continued, "we can't even think about a normal relationship. He's a conflict of interest. We're less than a week into the president's term, and I have this albatross hanging around my neck."

"You're saying it's not in your best interest to tell him?"
Gillian asked.

"Absolutely not."

"Never?"

"I can't picture it."

Gillian cocked her head, clearly pondering the facts of the
situation as she reached for another handful of nuts. "Then
what you need to do is sleep with someone else."

Cara thought she must have misheard. *"What?"*

"I don't mean literally. I mean, make it clear to Max that you
haven't been exclusive. When he finds out you're pregnant, he
might insist on a DNA test, but if he's not daddy material, he
might be content to let the matter drop. What he doesn't know
won't cost him anything."

Cara digested her sister's words. "You're very cynical."

Then she tried to picture the conversation where she casually informed Max that she'd been sleeping with other men
while they'd dated. No, not while they'd dated. That was dress-
ing it up too much. She meant while they'd tried and failed to
keep their hands off each other.

"I've been around a lot longer than you have," Gillian retorted.

"Fourteen months?"

"I've always been more worldly than you."

The waitress arrived, opening the bottle and pouring a glass
for Gillian. Cara refused and asked for a hot chocolate instead.

"So, you think it's okay for me to keep it from him? I mean
ethically?" Cara asked.

Gillian shrugged. "Why not?"

Cara leaned back, slouching more comfortably in the chair.
"That wasn't what I expected you to say."

"You thought I'd tell you to run to him, 'fess up and see if
he wanted a white picket fence and all the trimmings?"

Cara hated to admit it, but that was kind of where her
thoughts had been going. Not that she'd have agreed. Still, it

would have been nice to have some moral support for her out-
rageous fantasy.

"Oh, Cara." Gillian's face screwed up in pity. "That's not
good."

"No, that's not what I thought," Cara lied. "And that's not
what I want. The last thing I need is some miserable martyr of
a man, hanging around my house, trimming my hedges, cleaning my barbecue and blaming me for having ruined his daz-
zling career. Thank you, but no. I don't need that kind of grief."

Gillian was silent for a moment. "Well, you almost convinced me. But you might want to work on your delivery."

"Excuse me?"

"You protested a little too much there."

Cara hated to admit that Gillian was right. She knew Max
would never want them to be a family, but sometimes she just
couldn't help but wish for it herself.

Max and Jake listened with rapt attention while Liam Fisher
outlined some of the underhanded tactics ANS had used in
the past to track down big stories. The three men were at the
Apex Lounge at the topmost stop of the ski gondola. It was
lunchtime, and the facility was quickly filling up with fami-
lies and children.

"It became exponentially worse when that producer Marnie Salloway arrived," Liam was saying. "The woman has no
conscience. I'd be surprised if she has a soul."

"Do you have an example?" Max asked. Marnie was his
former boss, and he could well believe she was up to no good.
He and Jake had been working in Fields for three days now.
They'd undertaken countless interviews, all of which were
next to useless. They had hour upon hour of footage where the
townspeople praised the president and looked puzzled when
asked about Eleanor Albert.

"It went beyond manipulation," said Liam. "There was
downright coercion. I never passed on an envelope full of cash,

but I definitely wined and dined a few people, a five-star resort for a weekend, a three-hundred-dollar bottle of wine and then the carefully framed question to get just the right sound bite."

"That's not illegal," Max pointed out.

A young boy shrieked and rushed past the table with three of his friends, each of them bumping Max's elbow. Max glanced around for parents, or maybe an adult supervisor for the jamboree kids, but didn't see anyone paying the slightest attention to the hooligans.

Max cussed under his breath.

"That was a straw that broke my back," said Liam.

For a split second, Max thought he was talking about the unruly children.

"She, I mean Marnie, wanted me to hide a microphone in a victim's house. A teenage boy who was bullied by a sports team. She was convinced he'd exaggerated the problem and wanted to expose what she considered a conspiracy against a popular coach."

Jake scoffed in disgust, while Max drew back in absolute shock.

"You have got to be kidding me," Max spat.

"That's when I quit. Or when I was fired for insubordination, depending on whose story you want to believe."

Squeals of high-pitched laughter sounded from outside on the gondola deck. Max reflexively glanced up to see a mob of kids had gathered there. They were jostling for their snowboards, pushing and teasing, tossing each other's hats and gloves in the air.

"How can a person even think around that?" Max complained.

Jake laughed at him. "Chill out, Max. They're just having fun." Then he turned his attention back to Liam, getting serious once more. "You have any proof of this stuff?"

Max also focused on Liam.

"Just my word against theirs," said Liam. "But I haven't

delved too deeply before. Once I was out of there, I got on with my life. So, you never know what we might find out if we go looking."

"How do we start?" asked Max as the waitress cleared their plates. He handed her his credit card.

"I've got a few favors I can call in," said Liam.

"We're not quite done in Fields," said Max. "But we can meet you back in D.C."

Liam nodded his agreement. "Are you two boarding down now or taking the gondola?" asked Liam.

"I'm boarding," said Max, feeling the need to get some exercise and clear his head. Liam sounded like he was going to lead them in exactly the right direction, and Max knew things were going to get intense very soon.

Max raised his brow in a question to Jake, even though he already knew the answer. Jake would never take the easy way down.

"We'll meet you in the lobby," Jake told Liam with a grin.

Max signed the credit card slip and shrugged into his jacket as he headed for the exit.

Happily, most of the kids had vacated the deck. He assumed they were boarding their way down the hill. He could only hope they'd had enough of a head start to stay well ahead of him.

While Liam waited for the next gondola car, Max and Jake made their way to the rack that held their snowboards. Max's path to his board was blocked by a boy of about eleven who was struggling with his bindings.

Inwardly sighing at the delay, Max crouched down on one knee. "Need some help?" he asked, masking his frustration with a friendly tone.

He couldn't help but wonder where the kid's parents were or why a member of the jamboree staff or even the ski hill staff hadn't already assisted the boy. Max had seen numerous officials wandering the slopes in bright yellow jackets with the name of the hill plastered across the back.

"It's stuck," the boy whined, jamming at the buckle with his fingers.

Max looked at the kid's face and realized the boy was fighting back tears.

"Don't worry." He did his best to sound reassuring. "We can fix it up."

Stripping off his gloves, Max straightened a bent buckle on one of the mechanisms. Then he pulled the strap through, tightening it until it was secure.

"How does that feel?" he asked the boy.

The boy flexed his foot. "Okay." He sniffed.

Max straightened as Jake came up behind them, one foot secured to his board, the other pushing himself along the even ground.

As Max reached for his own board, he noticed the boy glancing worriedly around.

"Are you here with you parents?"

"My friends."

"Oh." Max glanced around for a likely looking group. "Can you see them?"

"They left." The boy pointed to the start of a medium-difficulty run. "That way."

"They left you behind?" *Nice friends.*

The boy nodded, looking both embarrassed and upset.

Moving a few feet to the top of the slope, Max strapped his boots to his board while Jake secured his free foot. This was really none of their concern. But it wasn't like they could leave the poor kid to his own devices.

"What's your name?" Max asked the kid.

"Ethan."

"Well, Ethan." Max snapped his goggles into place and did a quick check to make sure Ethan was all set to go. "I guess you'd better ride down with us."

The boy brightened.

"I'm Max, and this is Jake. I'm sure we can find your friends at the bottom."

As they headed down the run, it quickly became obvious that Ethan's enthusiasm outstripped his skills.

Max slowed his pace, pulling behind the kid, cringing at his sloppy technique and his wobbling balance. Ethan gamely tried to take a few, small jumps, but he took fall after fall on the landings.

Finally, Max couldn't stand it any longer. He pulled up beside him and helped him to his feet.

"Bend your knees," Max instructed. "Go back on your heels," he demonstrated. "But don't overbalance the landing. Here, hold out your arms, like this."

To his credit, Ethan watched carefully. He bit his lower lip and nodded in obvious determination.

"You want to watch me do it once?" asked Max.

"Yeah. That would be good."

"Okay." Max pointed to a small mound downhill from them. "That one."

He took it slow and easy, jumping just enough to get some air, exaggerating his balancing movements on the other side.

Ethan took a turn. Surprisingly, he kept his feet on the landing. He grinned at the accomplishment, punching a celebratory fist in the air.

Max chose another small one, and Ethan followed.

It was the longest run of his life, but when they came to a rest point midway, Ethan took the most impressive jump so far, getting a fair degree of air, then landing it and keeping upright.

Max found himself shouting in celebration, while Ethan sprayed up a small rooster tail of snow and grinned ear to ear.

The sound of cheering erupted beside them, and Max turned to see a group of six boys calling congratulations to Ethan.

"Nice ollie!" shouted one.

"Bangin'," called another.

"How'd you get so rad in the last hour?" asked a third, coming closer.

Head up, shoulders square, Ethan jerked his thumb in Max's direction. "This guy knows how to rip."

One of the boys peered up at him. "Aren't you that Max something? The crocodile-wrestling guy on TV?"

The group's interest swung to Max.

"That's me," Max admitted. He pulled off his glove to shake the boys' hands. "Max Gray."

"Awesome," someone whispered.

One of the boys elbowed Ethan. "Ethan, how d'you know Max Gray?"

Ethan suddenly seemed a little starstruck.

"We met up top," Max offered into the silence. "Took a ride down together."

Ethan seemed to find his voice. "Can you show us something else?"

Max glanced at Jake, who was clearly struggling not to laugh at his predicament.

"Sure," Max agreed fatalistically. Part of his job was being nice to the viewers. Though the viewers were generally quite a bit older than these.

He made his way down the rest of the mountain, stopping and starting, seven young boys in tow, each struggling to execute his instructions. He had to admit, it wasn't all bad. The kids were friendly and polite, and most of them made some improvement in the course of the run.

At the end, they met up with the broader jamboree group. Someone produced a marking pen, and he signed all the boy's helmets. Jake, of course, got footage of the whole thing. Max knew he was never going to hear the end of this.

"I heard some of the kids talking about him this morning in the lobby," Gillian said as she and Cara made their way along the shoveled sidewalk. It was shortly after noon, and they were checking out the restaurants along the street. "Said he taught them to snowboard yesterday. It was total hero worship."

"Are you sure it was kids?"

"Yes. I can tell the difference between ten-year-olds and twenty-year-olds. He signed their helmets. I don't see how he can hate kids that much."

"That doesn't sound like Max," Cara ventured.

"Maybe you're wrong about him," said Gillian.

"He told me himself that he didn't like children," Cara pointed out. There wasn't any ambiguity in Max's opinion about having a family. If he was teaching them to snowboard, it must have been under duress.

Gillian stopped in her tracks and pointed to the door of the Big Sky Restaurant. "Here?"

The upscale family restaurant advertised gourmet burgers, and Cara was starving. "Looks fine to me."

They entered to find it warm inside, with a big stone fireplace at one end and cushioned leather seats at generous-size tables. Gillian chose a half round booth and slid inside. Each of them snagged a menu.

"It must be the mountain air," said Cara.

Gillian grinned at her.

"Hey, you're hungry, too," Cara pointed out.

"Not as hungry as you."

Cara didn't argue the point. Instead her interest was snagged by pictures of burgers and fries.

"You'll have a whole new fan base after tonight," said a familiar voice next to their table.

Cara glanced up to meet Jake's surprised eyes.

"Cara," he greeted her with a smile. Then he looked at Gillian and his smile widened further. "And... *friend*. Do you ladies mind if we join you?"

"Please do," Gillian answered before Cara could find her voice.

"Hello, Cara." Max gave her a slight nod.

"New fan base?" asked Gillian as Jake took up the seat beside her.

"Young snowboard enthusiasts," Jake answered, holding his hand out to Gillian. "Jake Dobson, Max's cameraman."

"Gillian Cranshaw. Cara's sister."

"Not hard to guess you're related," said Jake, glancing from one woman to the other.

Max seemed to take his seat next to Cara rather reluctantly. "You sure you don't mind?" he asked.

"No problem." She could do this. She'd force herself to do this, coolly, casually, unemotionally.

They were both in Fields. It was a small town. For the next few days, she'd have to cope with running into Max. It was probably good practice.

She turned her attention back to the menu. "I think I'll have a milk shake," she mused, her sweet craving still out in full force. "Chocolate."

"Cara always did go wild at lunchtime." Gillian laughed.

"What about you?" Jake asked Gillian. "You ever get wild?" His intimate tone drew Cara's attention. Appreciation of Gillian's beauty was clear in his eyes.

Cara had seen that look from men a hundred times. Although she and Gillian looked very much alike, Gillian had always had a glamorous streak, a little more makeup, a little heavier on the jewelry, professional highlights in her hair, designer clothes and an eye for accessorizing that Cara admired.

Gillian rolled her eyes at Jake's interest, then she deftly shifted her attention to Max. "Nice to see you again, Max. The kids were all talking about you in the lobby this morning."

"No good deed goes unpunished," Max drawled.

"Did something happen?" asked Cara, glancing from man to man.

"Montana isn't the strongest market for *After Dark,*" Jake explained. "Max was hoping to stay a little bit under the radar."

"Not that you're helping me any," Max pointed out to Jake.

"I got some good footage yesterday. There's a chance editing can turn it into a sweet human interest story." Jake closed his menu. "It's not like we're getting anything on the president."

Cara looked at Max, curiosity piqued. "You don't say?"

"Don't give away our information," Max admonished Jake.

"Not blowing the case wide open?" Cara pressed Max.

"Too busy teaching small children to snowboard," he replied laconically as he perused the sandwich section of the menu. "And you?"

"Haven't been teaching anything to small children." She felt her arm drop reflexively to her lap.

Then Gillian smiled innocently over her menu at Max. "Do you have any children of your own?" she asked.

Cara nearly choked. Had her sister lost her mind?

Jake coughed out a hearty laugh. "Not Max. At least, none that he knows about."

Cara felt light-headed for a moment.

"No children," Max told Gillian in a firm voice. "You?"

"No children," Gillian responded. "No husband. No boyfriend."

"Really?" Jake angled his body toward her.

"Down, boy," Gillian put in, dropping her gaze to the open menu. "I think I'll go with a strawberry shake."

"I'm recently single myself," Jake told her smoothly.

"Quit hitting on Cara's sister," said Max.

"It's fine," Gillian assured Max with an impish smile that said she dealt with it all the time. Cara knew she did.

"You think this is hitting on her?" Jake asked in a mock-wounded tone. "Clearly, you've never seen me in action."

"I've seen you in action on six continents," Max replied. "I like Cara, and I don't want you messing with her family."

Gillian's gaze met Cara's. *He likes you,* was her silent message. *Makes no difference,* was Cara's message back. She and

Max were headed in completely different directions in life. They were already in opposing worlds, and no amount of liking each other was going to change that.

Five

They'd had to cut their lunch short. News that Max was in town had spread around Fields, and the level of attention on him continued to grow. Cara could tell that it frustrated him. And after the tenth polite but intrusive autograph request, they took their meals to go.

"We should head up to one of the hotel rooms," Jake suggested as they converged on the sidewalk.

"I'm in a closet," Cara responded. "The press office can't be extravagant with the taxpayers' money."

"I've got this suite thing on the top floor," said Gillian. "I take it we're hiding out?"

"I don't think I'm going to get any peace." Max frowned. "But the rest of you can do whatever you want." He looked a cross between brave and pathetic.

Cara shook her head. "Are you trying to be a martyr?"

"How'm I doing?"

"Poorly," said Cara.

"We're not going to abandon you," Gillian put in staunchly.

Cara wished her sister hadn't said that. Hanging out with Max seemed to send her on an emotional roller-coaster.

"Let's go to Max's villa," Jake suggested. "It's bigger than mine, and it's the highest one on the hillside. The place has a killer view, and if you want to wear off the milk shake, there's a path that leads to the hot springs."

"More like a goat track," Max put in. "Going down's not bad, but on the way up I kept wishing we had ropes and crampons."

"Works for me," Gillian said brightly.

Cara shot a sidelong glance at her sister. She sure hoped Gillian wasn't trying to throw Cara and Max together in the hopes that something sparked between them. If she was, the plan would definitely fail.

The men's SUV was closest, parked over in the hospital parking lot. Since it was starting to snow, and the road to the villas was slippery and steep, they all piled into the four-wheel-drive with Max at the wheel. The snow grew heavier as they approached the first of the villas. The local radio station was predicting six inches of new powder up in the peaks.

"I'm definitely taking a few runs tomorrow," said Jake from the backseat.

"As long as we can do it alone," Max put in. Then he glanced at Cara, who was sitting in the front passenger seat watching the big snowflakes splatter against the windshield. "I don't think I'm giving away any deep secrets if I tell you we're getting squat from our interviews."

"The most interesting footage I've taken this week was Max's snowboard lessons," said Jake. "Everything else was a waste of time and effort."

"What's not working for you?" Cara asked Max. From her perspective, things were terrific. She hadn't unearthed any time bombs that would hurt the president.

"Nice people saying nice things about what a nice boy the

president was as a teenager doesn't exactly make for riveting television."

"Just as I suspected." Cara couldn't keep the smug satisfaction from her voice. "You're going after the salacious story. You'd love it if you unearthed a scandal. No matter how detrimental to the country's governance or who you hurt."

The tires slid out beneath them, and Max wrestled the steering wheel to bring the vehicle back under control. "That's hardly fair."

"You want ratings, Max." It was no secret how the news media worked.

"My producer wants ratings," Max responded. "I want to know about Eleanor Albert."

"For the pure pursuit of knowledge, I'm sure."

"Well, I'm sure not going to cover anything up."

Oh, those were fighting words to Cara. "Are you implying that I will?"

The SUV automatically shifted to a lower gear, jerking everyone back in their seats.

"I'm implying that your loyalty is to the president." His gaze locked with hers.

"You're right about that." Her jaw tensed. Spending time with Max was an even worse idea than she'd imagined. "You should take us back to the hotel."

"No."

"Excuse me?"

"The burgers are already cold, and the milk shakes are already warm. And we're here." He skidded into a driveway and ratcheted the SUV into park.

"Maybe we could call a truce?" Gillian suggested from the backseat.

"The man's impossible," Cara ground out.

"He's just doing his job," Gillian responded.

Cara flashed her sister an annoyed glare. How dare she

be on Max's side? She opened her mouth to argue, but she stopped herself.

She didn't need to get petty to make her point. Max was doing his job. And Cara was doing hers. The conflict between them wasn't going to be resolved, and Gillian was going to figure that out very quickly.

"Fine," she agreed. "Truce."

Max didn't answer. But he did exit the vehicle, grabbing the bag of burgers.

Gillian came up beside her as they took the fieldstone staircase to the front door of the villa. "Are you trying to create a self-fulfilling prophecy?" she hissed in Cara's ear.

"What are you talking about?"

"You know how you get. He's a perfectly decent guy."

"He's a reporter who hates children."

"Right. I'm surprised he didn't throw those boys down the mountain, instead of, you know—"

"Yeah, yeah. I get it. He was nice to them, even though he didn't like them."

"I'm just saying, pay it forward for those young boys, be nice to their hero while he eats his burger. Can you do that?"

Cara could do that. She would do that. She was a professional. Then Gillian's other words echoed in her mind. "What do you mean 'how I get'?"

But Gillian skipped the last couple of steps to enter the villa. Max held the door, standing to one side, as Cara followed her sister inside.

The place was magnificent. Perched on the steep hillside, it had floor-to-ceiling windows across a two-story living and dining area. An archway at one end of the massive room led to a kitchen. On the opposite side of the foyer, was a large ski storage room, where they all hung their coats. A staircase led to an open second-floor hallway, which Cara presumed gave access to the bedroom. And beneath the bedroom, behind the living area, was a media room and a library.

"You can't see it through the falling snow," said Jake, "but the town is down there." He pointed. "And the lake is off to the south. You can see the highway winding away into the mountains. And if you go out on the balcony—"

"Pass," Gillian put in.

Jake smiled at her. "From the balcony, if you look north, you can see the lights from the ski runs at night."

"Clearly not the taxpayers' money," Cara muttered under her breath.

"I heard that," said Max, as Jake and Gillian moved off on an impromptu tour.

"Sorry," Cara responded, realizing Gillian was right. She was definitely being pricklier than usual.

"Let's eat," he suggested dryly, making his way to a dining table for eight.

"How many bedrooms?" Cara asked, forcing herself to be pleasant. She followed him and took up a chair facing the window.

She could easily imagine the view Jake had described. Though right now, it was turning into a wall of white. She'd been told about the sudden storms in the mountains and how they disappeared just as quickly as they came up, leaving miles and miles of champagne powder on the slopes.

"Just the one," said Max. "The villas are adults only. I think they cater to honeymoon couples and romantic weekends. Jake moved us up here when we discovered the jamboree down at the hotel."

"It must be nice and quiet."

"Very quiet." Max smiled. "And very nice."

Cara wanted to protest that kids weren't all bad. But instead she peeled the foil from her cheeseburger.

Max took a large bite of his and chewed. Then he wiped his mouth with a paper napkin. "Man, that's good."

Cara tasted her own burger and nodded in agreement. Lukewarm or not, the burger was delicious. She followed it up with a sip of her melting chocolate shake, and her stomach rumbled softly in appreciation.

If Max heard, he didn't comment. "Are you heading back to D.C. soon?" he asked.

"Likely tomorrow," she answered between bites.

"Same here. I don't think the story's in Fields, and we need to start prep work for South America."

"South America?" Cara prompted, popping a couple of cool fries in her mouth.

"We're going up into the Andes, looking at the impact of global mineral prices on exploration and on indigenous people." Max's jade-green eyes grew more intense as he spoke. "I'm particularly interested in the influence of China on local governments, labor standards and immigration."

She was struck, as she often was, by the depth of his understanding of his stories. He truly was a committed and ethical journalist. She felt guilty all over again for some of the accusations she'd tossed his way. "You're a very smart man, aren't you?"

"What I lack in intellect, I make up for in curiosity. I love a puzzle."

Cara didn't think Max was lacking anything in intelligence. She was beginning to agree with her sister. Her baby might have hit the genetic jackpot by having Max for a father.

"What about the president's paternity mystery?" she asked. "Does it make you curious?"

To her surprise, Max gave a careless shrug. He took a drink of his milk shake before answering. "Not really. Ariella's either his daughter or she's not. He either knew about it or he didn't. Neither case is going to fundamentally shift national policy in any way. And, honestly, I don't think Ariella's the story."

That statement surprised Cara. It worried her as well. "What is the story?" she couldn't help asking.

"You know I can't tell you that."

She knew that. Of course she knew that. Their entire relationship had centered around avoiding conflicts of interest. As a journalist, Max wasn't permitted to share his story angles with the White House press office.

She set down her burger, wiping her fingertips on the paper napkin. "I'm sorry I asked."

"It never hurts to ask."

"Yes, it does. It hurts to ask a question that puts someone else in an awkward position." She'd insisted he not do that with her, and now she was breaking her own rule.

"I'm a big boy, Cara." His expression went soft. "You don't scare me."

"You scare me plenty," she offered honestly.

"Okay, I can tell you this much."

"No, don't." She dramatically put her hands over her ears.

Jake's voice drawled as he and Gillian entered the room. "What is the man saying to you now?"

"Nothing," Cara quickly put in, removing her hands from her ears. "We were just joking around."

"You two?" Jake raised a brow. "I find that hard to believe." Then he glanced at the burgers and shakes. "Okay, this is sad."

"They're not bad," said Max, finishing his last bite.

"This from a man who once ate chocolate-covered ants." Jake looked to Gillian. "Believe me, you do not want to trust his opinion on cuisine."

"It was pretty good," said Cara, backing up her claim by polishing off the last bite of her own burger.

But Gillian frowned at the paper bag and cardboard cups. "Think I'll pass."

"Let's go grab something fresh," Jake suggested to her.

Cara started to protest, but her sister was nodding at Jake in agreement.

"We'll just be a few minutes," Jake promised, moving swiftly to the storage room, retrieving Gillian's coat and holding it out for her.

"What about the storm?" Cara tried, pointing out the window. Her next move was going to be to offer to go with them.

"It's letting up," said Gillian, allowing Jake to help her with her puffy white coat.

"We've got four-wheel drive," said Jake.

Gillian spoke directly to Cara. "You can stay here and play nice with Max."

Cara returned her sister's mischief with a glare. Gillian's not-so-secret plan was never going to work. No matter how nice Cara was to Max, he wasn't going to have an epiphany and realize he'd wanted to be a family man all along.

She started to rise. "I don't mind coming along for—"

"Not necessary," Jake put in. "Put up your feet. Finish your milk shake. The view's going to be spectacular in about fifteen minutes. We'll be back before you know it."

With that, they were out the door, leaving silence behind them.

"Do you think they wanted to be alone?" Max drawled.

Cara turned to him. "Huh?"

"It was pretty obvious."

That hadn't been Cara's read of the situation at all. She watched the black SUV back out of the driveway and head downhill. "You think?"

"Short of a neon sign, I don't think they could have made it any plainer."

No. Cara was pretty sure this was Gillian's not-so-subtle way of giving her some time alone with Max in the ridiculous and romantic hope that something would come of it.

"Sorry you got stuck with me," Max offered, watching her expression closely.

"I'm not stuck with—"

Okay, so she was stuck with Max. He definitely wasn't her first choice for a companion this afternoon. And it occurred to her that Jake and Gillian had left with the only vehicle. There was no escaping the villa until they returned. Good thing they were coming right back.

"Tell me more about South America." She forced herself to sit back in her chair and take the situation in stride.

Max's phone beeped, signaling that he had a text. He glanced at the screen.

"It's Jake."

"Already?"

"He wants us to turn on the local NCN news affiliate. It's five o'clock in D.C., and he wants to see if they run the snowboarding story."

"You don't look too happy about that," Cara observed.

"I don't like fluff."

"I thought it was the kids you didn't like." The words jumped out before she thought them through.

"Those, too," Max agreed.

Cara knew she needed to stop probing like that. Every time she asked a question about kids, he answered it honestly, and she felt even more depressed about her future.

While he located the TV remote control, Cara polished off the last of her fries and finished the milk shake. Normally, a burger and fries would have left her feeling stuffed. But she was still a little hungry. If this was the pregnancy affecting her, she'd have to be careful for the next nine months. It was embarrassing, but Gillian's abandoned burger was starting to look good.

Max located the NCN affiliate and turned up the volume. He sat down on one of two matching sofas. Cara moved to join him in the living room area, choosing an armchair that faced the television.

Sure enough, they ran with the story. Jake had even managed to get some sound of Max explaining the fundamentals of snowboarding and the kids cheering each other on.

The segment was brief, but Cara was astonished by Max's patience with the boys. It was clear they were in awe of him and just as clear that they were learning. Their techniques improved as they made their way down the slope. And, at the end, they were all obviously proud of their performance and overwhelmed by getting that kind of attention from a celebrity.

When Max signed everybody's helmets, she had to blink back a tear.

"Wow," said Max, shutting off the television. "That was quite the fluff piece."

Cara's emotion evaporated. "I thought it was nice."

"They'll milk it for suburban mom viewers, I guess," said Max.

"You looked like you were having fun." She couldn't bring herself to believe he'd hated it. She found her hand resting on her stomach again, and her mind started down the dangerous path of Max's suitability as a father.

"The whole time I was with them, I was wishing I could snowboard alone," he told her. "But they were viewers, so I had to behave. It'll never make the story. But given a choice, I'd have ditched the kids."

Well, that certainly put a stop to Cara's fanciful musings. "Are you saying it was all PR?"

"I'm saying that I'm not the saint the network would like me to be."

"So, you still don't like kids."

"There's a lot of real estate between liking kids and being friendly to the viewers. Just because I did my job, doesn't mean I'm going to become a grade-school teacher."

His phoned chimed, and he moved to the dining room table to retrieve it.

"Hey," he said simply.

Then he paused. "Right now?" Another pause. "Yeah, we'll be here. I'll tell her. Okay. Bye." He hung up.

"What is it?"

"Jake and Gillian won't be coming back right away, because Gillian had to get on a conference call."

Cara stomach fluttered. "Are you kidding me?"

"Apparently, it's morning in China, and the Chinese office needed to talk to her before the start of business. Her laptop is in her hotel suite, so they've gone back there."

"But…they…"

"Does that sound plausible to you?" Max asked, his face taking on a knowing expression. "Because I know Jake pretty well, and there's every chance they might be—"

"That's my *sister* you're talking about."

"Your sister doesn't have a sex life?"

"She's not sleeping with Jake." The two had only just met. "She has business interests in China, important business interests in China. I'm sure it's exactly what they say it is."

"Okay." Max held up his hands in surrender.

"I'm not blindly defending my sister's honor."

"You are, but that's admirable."

"I'm saying she does business with China."

"And I'm saying Jake is attracted to her."

"That doesn't mean the feeling is mutual."

Max returned to the living area. "We'll likely never know."

"I already know."

"You're cute, you know that?"

His smile sent an insidious warmth spreading through her body. It suddenly struck her exactly how foolish she'd been to let them end up alone.

"Max—" she began to protest, but then a rumbling sound distracted her. It was deep and low, a vibration as much as a sound.

Max's face blanched. He stiffened for a second then let out a guttural cussword. Before she knew what was happening, his arm was around her waist and he was dragging her.

"What?" she managed to sputter, even as the sound grew louder and the floor began to shake.

Max pulled her through the door to the bathroom, lifting her into the giant tub. "Lie down!" he commanded, disappearing.

They were having an earthquake. She'd never heard of a bathtub as a refuge place, but it seemed as good a place as any. She lay down.

In a few seconds, Max was back with her. He'd dragged the big square coffee table into the bathroom. He quickly lay down above her and put the table facedown over the tub.

The roaring grew to a piercing screech. The entire world was shaking around them. Cara reflexively clung to him, burying her face in his shoulder.

"Earthquake?" she managed in a hoarse voice.

"Avalanche." His arms tightened around her.

The lights flicked out, and the world turned murky gray.

"Are we still alive?" Cara's voice was barely a whisper in Max's ear.

The air had been silent around them for a full minute.

"We are," he answered, straining to hear any sounds around them.

"Is it over?"

"Maybe."

"Maybe?"

"One avalanche can trigger another." He kept his voice low, shifting onto his side to put her in a more comfortable position. In his rush to get her protected, he'd come down directly on top of her. "Am I hurting you?"

"No. I don't think so." She flexed. "Do we need to whisper?"

"No."

They both fell silent.

"How long do we wait?" she asked.

He slipped his fingers into the crack between the upside-down table and the tub, pushing the table aside. "I think we're okay."

He levered himself out of the tub, then turned to offer Cara his hand. She took it, and he hoisted her out, making sure she was steady on her feet.

His cell phone chimed from the living room.

Her voice held a slight tremor. "Do you think anybody was hurt?"

"I don't know." Max feared the worst.

His villa was still standing, but he'd experienced avalanches close-up before, and this had been a big one. The phone trilled again.

"You should get that," said Cara.

"You okay?"

She disentangled her hand from his. "I'm fine."

She looked pale but seemed all right.

He went after his phone, noting Jake's number.

"You guys okay?" Max said in greeting.

"Man, am I glad to hear your voice," said Jake. "How's Cara?"

"We're fine." Max watched as Cara came through the bathroom door. She paused to steady herself with a hand on the sofa back.

"They're fine," Jake informed someone at his end of the conversation. Max assumed it was Gillian.

"It must have just missed you," Jake said to Max.

"I haven't had a chance to look out. But I thought the villa was going to come off its foundation. What can you see from down there?"

"Half a mountainside covered in snow. The street is full of frightened people."

"Did it reach the town?"

"No. And the main slide didn't hit the ski hill."

"Thank goodness for that. Anyone hurt?" Max was itching to get into the fray. But there was no way off the mountain.

"Search and rescue is scrambling. But I don't think we're going to know anything for a while. You two okay where you are?"

"Sure," said Max. "The power's out, but we've got the fireplace."

"Judging from what I'm seeing here, you'll be there overnight."

"I guessed as much," said Max with a glance at Cara. Some of the color was coming back to her face. "Can you keep the two of us out of the news?"

"Sure," said Jake.

Max knew Cara wouldn't want anyone to know they were together. "I'm a little tired of being the story."

"Understood. I got some footage of it coming down. Had to use my tablet instead of a camera, but it looks like it came out okay."

Max couldn't help a half smile at that. Jake saw the world in video clips. While most people's reaction to danger was to wisely turn and run, Jake's reaction was to grab the nearest video recording device.

Jake wasn't finished. "If your phone battery's holding up, can you take a few minutes of footage from your vantage point?"

"I'll see what I can get."

"Can you put Cara on? Gillian wants to talk to her."

"Sure." Max moved to where Cara was sitting and held out the phone. "Gillian."

Cara seemed to brace herself. "Hello?"

She listened for a moment. "Yes. I am." Another pause. "Not a scratch. Well, maybe a little shell-shocked." Then she gave a nervous laugh. "Really?"

Curious to see what had happened outside, Max headed onto the snowy balcony, pulling the door closed behind him.

The scene around him was surreal. The bulk of the slide had fallen to the north of the villa complex. It had created a jagged slope of solid packed snow. The edge of it had stacked up against the side of the villa. Max knew from experience it would be hard as concrete.

Max and Cara weren't the only ones who'd been incredibly lucky in avoiding the disaster. The rest of the villas were south of Max's, farther down the hill. To that side, the slide paths were smaller, narrow, crashing their way through ravines and gullies, sticking to the low ground and, from what Max could see, missing the buildings.

He heard the door slide open behind him.

"Oh, my—"

He turned to where Cara had stopped dead in the doorway, staring at the moonscape beside the villa.

"The road's gone," she stated in astonishment, remembering to come outside and close the door behind her.

"It'll take a while to dig that out."

She moved up beside him at the rail. "Are we stranded?"

"For now. They could send a helicopter for us. But they probably don't have all that many resources, and the injured have to be their priority."

"Of course," Cara agreed. "Gillian said she offered them the use of her jet. They may need to evacuate some of the injured people to bigger hospitals and bring in more rescuers."

"It'll be dark soon," Max couldn't help observing. He sure hoped nobody was stranded on the ski hill in all this.

Cara shivered as she focused on the setting sun.

"We should go inside." His instinct was to put an arm around her shoulders. But he quickly stopped himself.

She'd been firm on the boundaries of their relationship, and he couldn't discount the possibility of telescope lenses trained on the avalanche damage picking them up.

"We really should go inside," he repeated.

If there was any chance of prying eyes, he wanted Cara out of sight. The fewer people who knew she was with him, the better off she'd be.

This time, she turned. He swiftly moved to pull open the sliding glass door, letting her through first.

With the power out, it was going to get cold and dark inside the villa very soon. He was guessing other people were trapped at other villas, but they were spaced too far apart for him to know for sure. At least he hadn't seen any villas with obvious structural damage. That was a good sign.

There was newspaper, matches and firewood next to the big stone fireplace. He'd also noticed two oil lamps on the mantel, and candles were placed at various spots around the room.

He lit the oil lamps, then handed the matches to Cara, keeping one for himself. "You want to look around and light a few candles?"

"Sure." She took the matches from his hand.

He knew it was better to keep her busy. If she stood around thinking about their close call, there was still a chance she could go into shock.

While she moved around the room, he crouched down on one knee and began laying a fire.

Luckily, the villas seemed well-prepared for a rustic lifestyle. Either they'd done it for the ambiance or power outages were common up here. But he knew there was a larger wood box at the back of the storage room. They'd be fine overnight, for a few days if it came to that.

He lit the newspaper, watching as flames curled up around the smaller pieces of kindling. "Your sister has a jet?" he opened.

"Her company has a jet."

"But she owns the company."

"That she does." Cara had lit half a dozen candles, and the room was filled with a soft glow of yellow light.

"Is it a big company?" Max added a couple of larger pieces to the fire. Satisfied with the crackling sound and the height of the flames, he closed the glass doors, adjusting the damper to the open position.

"It gets bigger all the time." Cara handed back the matches, and he put them on the stone mantel.

"Define *bigger*." He gestured to the sofa directly across from the fireplace. They might as well make themselves comfortable. Then he gave a laugh at his own question. "I guess it's big enough to buy a jet."

"One of their software applications has been widely adopted by the international health-care industry. Since that started, I think the sky's the limit." Cara settled into one corner of the sofa.

Max gave a low whistle as he took up the other end of the couch. "Successful family you've got going."

"I think that depends on who you ask."

"A member of the White House staff and an IT entrepreneur? Under what benchmark is that not successful?"

"Rural Wisconsin."

"Wisconsin has something against high tech?"

"If my parents had their way, Gillian and I would have found ourselves a couple of nice dairy farmers, settled down in the Rim Creek area and started producing grandchildren."

"Ahh." Now he understood.

"Fortunately for everybody, my brother found a wonderful local girl and fell in love. She's pregnant with their third at the moment, and they seem perfectly happy living on the farm."

"Farm life's not for you?"

Cara gave an exaggerated shudder. "Gillian and I couldn't wait to leave."

Then, unexpectedly, she smiled. "When I was in fifth grade, Gillian studied with me every night. We had a secret plan for me to skip grade six so we'd graduate the same year, and we could go off to college together."

"Did it work?"

"Not that year. But I got far enough ahead that I was able to take extra classes in high school and finish early."

Max couldn't help but be impressed. "So it did work."

"Eventually. We left together for Milwaukee. After a couple of years, I switched to Harvard, and she went to MIT."

He couldn't help taking in Cara's fresh-faced beauty in the firelight. The young men of Rim Creek must have been very disappointed when she left. "You'd have made a cute dairy-maid."

"I'd have failed miserably."

"Funny how you grew up in the country and ended up in the big city. I grew up in the middle of the city and ended up craving the wilderness."

She glanced around. "You must love this."

He did. But not for the reasons she meant. They were all alone for the entire night, and his imagination was working overtime on the implications.

Six

Candlelight bounced off the polished cherrywood table. The leather dining chairs were deep and luxurious, the fire crackled and popped in a soothing backdrop and the expensive crystal and china shone in the flickering light.

The only thing out of place was the instant oatmeal where a five-star dinner should have been. Cara's was apple cinnamon, while Max had gone with maple sugar.

Cara wasn't about to complain. Though they had no power and no heat, Max had dug out the propane barbecue on the balcony. He'd cleaned it up, got it running and boiled some water in the kettle. The hot water, along with the few provisions in the villa's kitchen, had yielded both oatmeal and tea. Left to her own devices, she wouldn't have had even that much.

Jake had sent another message from town, with the encouraging news that a group of children with only minor injuries had been rescued from one of the slopes. Work would go on all night, bringing stranded people down from the Apex Lounge at the top of the gondola. Cara had texted her boss, letting them all know she was safe, but with the warning that she was conserving the battery in her phone.

She and Max had then shut down their communication devices, and now, except for the distant glow of the town below, they were cut off from the world.

"You really were a Boy Scout," said Cara, as she blew gently on a first spoon of oatmeal.

"What makes you say that?" Max was seated directly across from her at one end of the long table. She had a view out the glass wall at the far end, and heat from the living room fire warmed her back.

"You lit the fire. You thought to use the barbecue to boil the water. I bet you know first aid and how to whittle."

"Yes to the first aid, but there weren't a lot of Boy Scouts in my neighborhood."

Cara knew Max had grown up in south Chicago, and she knew his single mother had worked as a waitress. "So how did you learn all that?"

"Trial and error. Mostly error. While I was in college, I took some adventure vacations, embarrassed myself, nearly got people killed. When you grow up in a basement apartment without so much as a hammer or a screwdriver, never mind camping equipment or a father to show you how they're used, you hit your eighteenth birthday with a bit of a handicap."

Cara was sorry she'd asked. "I didn't mean—"

"I'm not upset with you. I'm not upset with anybody. Life is what it is sometimes. I can't control how I grew up. I can only control what I do from here on in."

She knew she shouldn't ask, but she couldn't help herself. "Is that why you don't want a family? Because of your bad memories?"

"There are a lot of reasons why I don't want a family. Experience, yeah. I wouldn't wish my childhood on anyone. And I wouldn't wish my mother's life on anyone. Every single day of her life was a grind."

"Poverty was a big part of that," Cara pointed out.

Max didn't respond to her comment. "Don't even get me started on genetics," he said. "I'm the product of a father who was willing to walk out on the mother of his child, walk out on his own son, walk out on his responsibility. You think the world needs more people from that particular gene pool?"

"You're not like him."

"Oh, yes, I am. I'm here today, but I'll be gone tomorrow. I may use a jet plane instead of a bus, but I'm living in my own, selfish world, following my own, selfish dreams."

"But you're not leaving anyone behind." Cara knew it was a completely different situation.

"Exactly," Max agreed. "That's the beauty of the system. I'm not hurting anyone. I could get shot and killed in a conflict zone or swept down a waterfall and drown and it wouldn't matter one little bit."

"It would matter."

"Yeah, well, NCN's ratings might drop. But that would be a temporary "

"Your *friends* would miss you." She couldn't stand to hear him talk that way. He was loved and respected by his friends, his peers, even his viewers.

"Hey, I don't mean that as a bad thing. I mean it as a source of freedom. Of course my friends would miss me. If they died, I'd miss them, too. But losing a friend is nothing compared to losing parents or a spouse. I'm not going to be the guy who leaves loved ones behind to fend for themselves."

"Let me get this straight. You're protecting your potential wife and your potential children by never allowing them to exist?"

Max gave a thoughtful nod. "Yeah, that's pretty much it."

"There's something wrong with that logic." More than she would tell him. More than she could ever tell him.

"Not from where I'm sitting."

"You can't live in a bubble, Max."

She tried to tell herself that none of this was a surprise. She'd known all along Max wasn't father material. He wasn't even relationship material. She had no right to get all maudlin now just because he'd laid it out in no uncertain terms.

Nothing had changed in the last five minutes. She still had a couple of months before she'd even have to hide her pregnancy. She'd decided to ask Lynn about an international posting. There was an ongoing need for communications support in the embassies. She'd like London, or maybe Sydney, or even Montreal. Her child could learn French while he or she was growing up.

"I'm not living in a bubble," Max countered. "I jump out of airplanes, climb mountains, ford rivers. I even wrestled a crocodile once."

"Ah, the infamous crocodile story." She forced herself to lighten things up, taking another bite of her oatmeal.

"Okay," he said. "In the interest of full disclosure—but I warn you, what happens while trapped by an avalanche, stays in the avalanche."

She managed a smile at that. "Good grief, what are you about to confess?"

"My guide on that trip? He was nearby in the boat. And I think, well, I know, he conked the gator on the head with his paddle before the wrestling match started."

Cara worked up a censorious frown, her tone clearly disapproving. "Are you saying the crocodile was incapacitated?"

"I'm guessing. But Jake got the footage, and we all kind of agreed to pretend it was a bigger deal than it was."

"You fought a punch-drunk crocodile?"

"And won."

"And parlayed it into the he-man, adventurer reputation you now enjoy amongst your innocent and apparently duped fans."

There was a twinkle in his eye. "I never claimed to be a Boy Scout."

"Okay. I guess I'm in no position to be snooty. I've never wrestled any kind of crocodile."

"Just the vultures in the press."

"Some days, I wish somebody would clonk them on the head with a paddle."

Max turned thoughtful. "There's nothing in Fields for either of us. I mean about Eleanor."

Her guard went up. "You know I can't discuss that with you."

"I'm not asking for information. I'm just making an observation. Nobody's talking. Nobody admits to remembering anything of significance. Which means either there's a conspiracy going on here worthy of the CIA or people truly don't remember."

"I think they don't remember," Cara put in before she could stop herself.

"I agree," Max returned. "And doesn't that beg the question of how Angelica Pierce and ANS found the story?"

Cara had to agree that it did. "Do you have a theory?"

Max leaned slightly forward. "Are you offering quid pro quo on an information exchange?"

"You know I can't do that."

"Then I don't have a theory." He paused. "Except that I do. And it's a good one."

It was her turn to lean forward. "You're bluffing."

"Only one way for you to find out."

There were, in fact, two ways for her to find out. But the second one was worse than the first.

"I can tell what you're thinking," he taunted.

"No, you can't."

"You're thinking that if you got naked, I'd tell you anything."

"I am *not* going to bribe you with sex."

He seemed to consider that. "Too bad. Because it'd work."

* * *

Max knew he had to keep himself busy for the rest of the evening. Because if he let his attention get stalled on Cara, he'd go stark, raving mad.

He'd cleaned up the dishes, refilled the wood box and checked the walls for damage where the avalanche snow had piled up. Now he was methodically working his way through the drawers and cupboards in the living area, looking for anything that might be useful to them if they were stuck here for a couple more days.

Cara had hung her blazer in the closet, commandeered a fuzzy robe from the powder room to help her keep warm and borrowed a pair of Max's socks to use as slippers. She should have looked comical, curled up in a corner of the sofa with a magazine in her hand, but she was sexy.

"What did you find?" she called across the room, having noted he was staring vacantly into the bottom of a cabinet.

He stopped himself from turning to look at her again. "Board games." He pulled one out at random. "Monopoly?"

"I haven't played that in years."

"What do you play? *Angry Birds?*" he asked her.

She laughed. "Angry voters."

He couldn't help but smile at that. "Are you winning?"

"Hardly ever."

He came to his feet, Monopoly game in hand. "Care to take me on?" He was about to run out of busywork, and concentrating on Monopoly was better than concentrating on Cara.

"I thought I was already taking you on," she returned. But she closed the magazine and set it on the table.

He decided to take that as a yes.

He made his way to the dining room table, moving a couple of candles to one side, then opened the old box to see if enough of the pieces were there to play a game.

Surprisingly, the contents seemed mostly intact, if a bit dog-eared and faded.

Cara pulled up a chair. "Is the dog there?"

"We have the dog." Max unfolded the board between them and handed her the game piece.

"What are you taking?" she asked, reaching for the piles of colored money and starting to sort.

"Top hat," he decided.

"Not the race car?"

He frowned. "It looks like an import."

"You're an American muscle car guy?"

"That's right. Nothing quite like touring a Mustang GT convertible out on Route 1." He got comfortable in the chair across from her, then located the dice and stacked the game cards in their respective piles.

Cara paused, her blue eyes going dreamy. "That sounds nice."

"I'll take you anytime you want to go. Well, we might want to wait for April or May. Unless we start in Georgia." In the winter, he always used a hardtop.

"You have a convertible?"

"I have three."

"You don't think that's a little excessive?"

"They're part of my collection."

She gave him a knowing smile. "In my book, 'collection' is merely a justification for excess."

"No argument from me."

She looked him straight in the eye. "Now there's a first."

"Ouch," he told her softly.

"How many cars do you own?"

Max did a quick calculation in his head. "Seventeen. But three of them are in the middle of restoration work. Most of them are vintage."

"You restore old cars?"

"I do."

"How come I didn't know this?"

"There are many things you don't know about me."

"But where? How? You live in a penthouse on Connecticut Avenue."

"I also have a house in Maine."

"Seriously?"

"Why would I make that up?"

She went back to sorting the money. "I'm just surprised. You've never mentioned it before."

"Cara, we haven't had that many dates." And most of their time alone together had been spent debating the political issues and events of the day. Or in bed. They'd spent an awful lot of their time alone together in bed. Which might explain his rather Pavlovian urge to kiss her right now.

Her hand slowed in the money sorting, then came to a stop on the stack of fifties. She looked up at him, and he could see the same thoughts making their way through her brain.

"What else don't I know about you?" she asked.

"Many, many things. Most of them good."

Her mouth twitched in a smile. "Tell me the bad ones."

"You first."

She drew back in what was obviously mock affront. "There's nothing bad about me."

"You've got the hots for a maverick, daredevil news reporter."

"Ha. Me and about a million other women."

"Thanks for the compliment." He gave her a nod. "But you're different, and you know it."

"I'm not different. I'm exactly like all those other women who run panting after the famous, sexy crocodile wrestler."

"You're different to me," he told her honestly.

"Only because I'm the one in front of you at this moment."

"Beautiful women are in front of me all the time. I don't feel this way about them."

"Then it's because you can't have me."

Max had considered that. In fact, he'd considered it quite a lot. Could the fact that Cara was off-limits make her even more appealing? Was it possible his mind was playing tricks on him? Was it possible he was that shallow?

"It's true," she crowed triumphantly at his silence.

"I sometimes wish it was," he returned. "It would make things a whole lot easier."

She tapped her index finger on the table. "If I was available. If I was, I don't know, let's say a bank manager. If I was nobody in public or political life. If I'd confessed my passionate, undying love for you and told you I wanted to spend the rest of my life with you, marry you, have your babies—"

"What?" Everything inside him recoiled. "Where did that come from?"

She shook her head. "You don't want me, Max."

"I don't see going from zero to a hundred in two seconds flat. I don't see pretending you're a completely different person than you are. If you were you, but had stayed on the dairy farm and were looking for a hick, hayseed husband to read *Farming Today* and escort you to the barn dance on Saturday night, I wouldn't have fallen for you."

"Well, aren't you shallow."

"But you're not that. You'd never be that. I like you just the way you are, Cara. In your current life. In your current circumstances. With your current hopes and dreams and value system."

"Where I'm the forbidden fruit."

"It's more complicated than that."

"You have no idea."

He reached across the table and covered her hand with his. "I have a very, very good idea. You and I are trapped in separate worlds. Those worlds are incompatible."

Her gaze locked on to their hands. "I'm glad to know you've been listening."

He squeezed her hand, and she didn't fight him.

"Come here," he told her softly.

"No."

"Then I'll come there." He rose and rounded the end of the dining table.

"Max." She sighed in obvious frustration.

But he took her hand again, drawing her to her feet.

She looked confused and vulnerable. "I have to protect myself from you."

"You're doing a terrific job."

"No, I'm not."

"But not tonight. You don't need to stay away from me tonight."

"Max—"

"It's just you and me, Cara. For the first time, maybe the one and only time, our lives beyond these walls are irrelevant."

"I can't—"

He put a finger across her lips. "I'm not asking for state secrets or any other kind of information. You can stop talking right now and not say another word until morning if you want."

She rolled her eyes at that.

He grinned. "That's not how I meant it, and you know it." Then he sobered, moving closer, inhaling deeply, letting her scent waft over all his senses. "For now, and only for right now, I'm simply Max and you're simply Cara. That's not going to happen again for another four years."

"Eight years," she corrected around his finger.

"That's even worse."

"Not for President Morrow."

"Do you want to be serious?"

"No. Absolutely not. I can't stand here and reasonably, logically rationalize sleeping with you tonight."

"You're overthinking, Cara."

"It's better than underthinking."

He tipped his head toward her. "Forget thinking. I'm kissing you now."

"Max," she protested softly.

It wasn't a no, he told himself. Maybe he was the one rationalizing now, but she definitely hadn't said no.

When Max's lips touched hers, Cara all but melted in the firelight. His strong arms enveloped her, pulling her tight, bringing her home. His scent was familiar, as was the pressure of his full lips, the tease of his tongue and the way his hands roamed her back, as if he needed to press every individual inch of her body against his own.

She told herself one minute, then two, then three. But Max's embrace was the best place in the world to be. He was her biggest weakness and her hopeless addiction.

He whispered against her mouth, "I've missed you so much."

He tugged the sash of her robe, his gaze penetrating hers as he pushed it off her shoulder, spreading it on the thick carpet in front of the fire. He flicked the buttons of her white blouse, one by one, until he revealed her lacy bra.

She reached for his tie.

The breath whooshed out of his body as she worked the knot. Then he stood still as she pushed his shirt buttons through their buttonholes.

The fire flickered on his tanned body, highlighting the half-dozen scars that marred his chest. She traced the longest one with her finger, and he sucked in a breath.

"Hurt?" she asked softly.

"Not at all."

She traced another. "Gator?"

"Tree branch. Parachute landing." His thumbs stroked across her midriff, teasing the skin beneath her breasts. "You are so soft, so perfect."

"That's because I don't jump out of airplanes." She stretched up for another kiss.

"Don't ever get hurt."

She had no idea how to respond, so she kissed him instead.

"I couldn't stand it if you got hurt." He deepened the kiss, pushing her blouse from her shoulders, letting it drop to the floor. The fire crackled in the quiet room, warming the air, scenting it with the light fragrance of cedar smoke.

She discarded his shirt, and he deftly removed her bra. Then he wrapped her in his arms once again, skin to skin. She let her fingertips trail down his strong back. Giving in to impulse, she feathered kisses along his chest, tasting his skin, drawing his essence into her mouth.

His hand cupped her breast, and pulsing desire skipped its way to every corner of her body. Her hands convulsed against his back.

He eased her down to the floor, laying her gently on her back against the thick robe. The villa was cooling with the night, but the fire was warm on one side and Max's body radiated heat on the other. He leaned up on one elbow. His index finger traversed a line from her neck to the tip of her shoulder. He moved over one breast, then down to her navel.

"How can you be so beautiful?" he asked as his explorations moved back higher.

He grazed the tip of her nipple, sending waves of pleasure through her body, tightening her muscles, making her spine reflexively arch.

He did it again, and her eyes fluttered closed. Then he moved to the other breast, and she felt a wash of heat and desire suffuse her skin. Goose bumps rose, and a pulse began to throb low in her belly.

He released the button of her slacks, easing down the zipper and quickly stripping them off.

Her body rife with growing arousal, she reached blindly for him.

"Lie still," he whispered in her ear.

She complied, only because her bones had gone limp and it seemed like the easiest thing to do.

"I could watch you all night long." His words made her open her eyes.

His expression was intent as his hands moved along her thighs, over the white lace of her panties, skimming the jut of her hip bone, up to the indentation of her waist.

He had beautiful green eyes, a strong chin, a chiseled nose and dark lips that she knew were near magic. Every woman in D.C. was attracted to him. Yet he was staring at her with reverence.

He teased the edge of her panties, fingers dipping beneath, finding her smooth, sensitive skin. Her back arched again, eyes closing, hands curling into involuntary fists.

"Kiss me," she rasped.

She felt him bend toward her.

She parted her lips.

But instead of tasting him, she felt his hot mouth cover her nipple. He drew it inside his mouth, tongue curling around the bud. She groaned with pleasure, one hand moving to his head, grasping tight to his dark hair.

He switched to the other breast, and the fire seemed to grow hotter. She was awash with pleasure mixed with an urgent desire. Her thighs twitched apart, primed and ready for his touch.

"Max, please," she choked out, struggling to speak around the roar in her brain.

He kissed her swollen lips, and nothing had ever felt so satisfying. His mouth opened hers, and his tongue plunged deep, over and over again.

Without breaking the erotic kiss, he stripped off her panties. He kicked off his own pants. And then he was on top of her, his satisfying weight pressing her into the carpet. She was surrounded by heat from all sides.

She kneaded his back, his buttocks, widening her thighs, urging him in.

He eased up on his elbows, brushing her mussed hair from her face, trapping her gaze with his. "There's nobody else in the world," he told her. "Nobody."

He was quick with a condom. Then he kissed her lips and

flexed his hips. Her body welcomed him in. Her legs wrapped around him, her hips tilting up. There was nobody else in the world for her, either. She couldn't imagine these feelings, this connection, coming around more than once in a lifetime.

Tonight was precious. Tonight Max was hers. She curled her body around him and hung on tight. Time and space disappeared as his rhythm pounded reality from her brain.

His broad hand found the small of her back, pulling her up, holding her to him, rocketing shock waves of pleasure to every corner of her being.

She cried out his name, and he kissed her hard and deep. Her body bucked, and her world exploded over and over again.

She sucked in gulps of air, as the world slowly righted itself again. Max's breathing was ragged in her ear. He firmed his hold on her, carefully rolling them both so that she was on top. The fire crackled beside them, sending curls of warmth across her damp, bare back.

"That was…" she began. But she didn't have the first clue what to say after that.

"It was," Max agreed. "It truly was."

Streaks of dawn stretched pink across the overcast sky, the light revealing the snowy mountain peaks behind the villa. In the king-size bed on the second floor, Max kept his breathing even, his arms still and easy where they wrapped around Cara. She was asleep, her naked body spooned in front against his, and he didn't want to disturb her.

They were toasty warm beneath the covers. But the fire had gone out hours ago, and the villa was rapidly cooling off. The cold was like reality. They could stave it off for a little while, but eventually, they'd have to face it.

Cara stirred in his arms; the movement sent a fresh wave of desire through his body.

"Is it morning?" she asked, tone husky with sleep.

"Close." He gave in to impulse and pressed his lips against the back of her neck.

"Thanks," she murmured.

"Anytime." He kissed her again, lingering.

A laugh burbled up from her chest. "I meant for last night."

"Even better."

"For being here. The fire, the tea, the oatmeal. For knowing what to do and how to do it."

"I get that a lot." He slid his palm up her smooth stomach. "What to do…" He cupped the curve of her breast. "How to do it."

She trapped his hand. "I was about to say you were a knight in shining armor."

"And you're the maiden in distress? I can work with that."

"You're blowing it, Sir Max."

He shifted so that she rolled onto her back and he could look into her face. "Where you couldn't be doing better, fair Cara."

She shook her head but was obviously fighting a smile.

"Call me Sir Max again," he cajoled.

That got him a feeble smack on the shoulder.

He laughed and wrapped her in his arms, rolling once more so that she lay full on top, the length of her naked body pressing against his.

"You need to be serious," she told him.

He sobered. "No problem." He cradled her face, urging her forward, kissing her once, then again, then deeper.

She resisted at first, but within seconds she was returning his kiss. Her body turned pliant on his, molding around him.

He inhaled her scent, reveled in the softness of her skin, tasted her sweet mouth and let his fingertips absorb the texture of her silky hair. Passion arced the length of his body, bringing it to life. His hands were itchy to explore, and they slipped to her neck, over her smooth shoulders, to the small of her back, over her buttocks to the seam of her sculpted thighs, to—

She groaned against his mouth.

He stilled. "Too soon? Sore?"

"No." She shook her head. "Well, yes. But no. Not enough to…"

He struggled to keep himself still while she made up her mind, his muscles twitching with anticipation, a pulse beginning to throb inside his ears. She was wet and hot and sweet, and he could only hover on the brink for so long.

She drew slowly back a few inches. "Max?" Her voice was breathless.

"Yeah?" he managed, his free hand curling into a fist.

"You have to promise me something."

Anything, anything, *anything.* "Now?"

"It's—"

He moved his hand, and she sucked in a breath.

"Good or bad?" he asked.

Her eyes fluttered closed, and her mouth dropped open, her back arching into his hand.

He was taking that as good. He leaned up to kiss her, drew her down to meet him and pushed everything else to the back of his mind. His body took over, mouth roaming, hands ranging. He turned her onto her back, settling between her legs.

She was all motion beneath him, her fingertips digging into his back, her kisses deep and passionate. She suckled his neck, dampening his skin, her breath then cooling the spot. Her hand moved between them, her thighs parting, her fingertips closing around him, guiding him.

"Condom," he managed as some scrap of sanity dredged up from the base of his brain.

But she kept going. "It's fine. It's good." She sucked in a couple of deep breaths. "So good," she groaned.

In reaction, his hips flexed. Her heat engulfed him, and there was no going back. He fought to measure his pace, his mind telling him to go slow, while his body strained to gallop forward.

They were a perfect fit, a perfect rhythm, and she breathed

his name over and over in his ear. He buried his face in her neck, planting wide-open kisses, reveling in the salty tang of her skin, likely leaving marks.

Her spine arched, her neck stretched and her hips bucked up against him. Passion boiled in his body, obliterating everything but Cara.

He groaned her name and felt her hot, damp body convulse around his. He fell over the edge to oblivion.

Max took long, deep breaths, his limbs like jelly, his weight pressing Cara into the soft mattress. He decided he must be getting old, because it sure shouldn't take him this long to recover from lovemaking.

"Max?" Her tone was hollow against his ear.

"Am I squishing you?"

She shook her head. "Don't move."

"Okay."

"You feel good."

"I feel amazing." He felt like he'd been drugged, in a good way, in a way that could make him an instant addict.

"You have to promise me something," she told him, voice still quiet and husky.

Right. He remembered now. He'd interrupted her. Or she'd interrupted him. Clearly, it was something important.

"For the president?" he asked.

"For me."

Regaining just enough strength to operate his arms, Max lifted up on his elbows. "For you? Anything." He meant it. Procedure be damned. Protocol be damned. Laws be damned. If Cara needed something from him, he'd move heaven and earth to make it happen.

She moved her gaze away from his. "When they get here… When we're rescued and we go back to D.C.…."

"I'm not telling anybody anything," he pledged. What had happened between them was personal and private. It had no bearing on their professional lives, and it was nobody's business but their own.

"I need you to stay away from me."

He didn't like it. But he understood. They disagreed on how their relationship could work while the president was in office. He got that. And he wouldn't presume that last night changed anything.

"I know how you feel," he began.

But she put a finger across his lips to silence him. "I mean it, Max. You have to stay away from me, completely away. I'm not strong enough to fight you. You'll win. And you winning will be very, very bad for me."

"There's nothing that says we can't be friends."

She glanced down at their naked, entwined, joined bodies. "We can't be friends, Max."

He felt as if he'd been sucker punched. He wasn't ready to say he'd wait four years for her. But he wasn't ready to say he wouldn't. He didn't know where this was going. But she didn't, either, and they couldn't just walk away.

"Promise me," she pressed, capturing his gaze. "No more dropping by my apartment. No more seeking me out at events. No more leaving your watch behind."

"No." No way, no how. She was entitled to her perspective, but he had a right to make his case.

A sheen formed in her eyes, and he felt like the worst jerk in the world.

"You have to let me try." There was a pleading tone in his voice.

She blinked. "If you try, I'll get hurt."

"I won't hurt you, Cara." He found himself gathering her close again, voice rumbling with emotion. "I swear I won't hurt you."

There was a catch in her tone. "Stay away, Max. If you care about me at all, then stay away."

Max felt a block of ice settle into his chest. He'd sworn he'd do anything for Cara. And this was the thing she asked of him. For that reason, it was what he'd do. He'd do it for her. Even if it killed him.

Seven

It had been midmorning when the snowmobiles arrived at the villa to rescue them. Cara used the helmet and a scarf to camouflage her identity as they headed back into town. But it turned out she needn't have bothered. The town was busy, people focused on repairs to the ski runs and on the final rescue activities. A few fingers pointed at Max when he dismounted and removed his helmet. But Cara was far across the parking lot, being shadowed by a different rescuer, and it didn't seem to occur to anyone they might have been together.

Thankfully, she quickly learned that everyone was accounted for. Those with injuries had been taken to the Fields medical center, with a few of the more serious cases shipped to hospitals in larger towns nearby. All were expected to recover.

Cara had met up with Gillian in the lobby of the hotel and learned that Jake was taking Max out to cover the avalanche story. Cara, on the other hand, was needed back in D.C. So they packed and made their way to the airport.

There was no excuse for her to stay in Fields any longer.

But as Cara climbed the narrow staircase to Gillian's jet, she felt like she was leaving something precious behind. She knew her mind was playing tricks. What she was sad to leave was a fantasy where Max was a perfect husband and father. The reality was something altogether different, and she was going to have to get used to that.

She ducked her way through the jet's door, inhaling the soft scent of new leather. The dozen white seats looked more like armchairs than airplane seats, each pair facing one another with a polished rosewood table between. Near the back was a sofa, oriented sideways, across from an entertainment center. Burgundy throw pillows gave a decorator's touch, and large, oval windows illuminated the pale interior.

Cara made her way to one of the luxurious seats in the forward half of the cabin. The copilot had relieved her of her luggage, and she tucked her purse beside the seat as she sat down.

"Did you turn into a billionaire when I wasn't looking?" she asked her sister.

Gillian grinned from the doorway. "Not yet." Then she turned to speak to the pilot, her voice too soft for Cara to hear.

"Yet?" Cara prompted as Gillian moved toward her.

"Maybe someday. Well, really, depending on how things go in India," said Gillian as she plunked down across from Cara. "Fingers crossed. If you're curious, I can check with my accountant and see how close we're getting."

The hydraulics whirred as the jet plane door folded into the closed position.

"Do you ever stop and let it boggle your mind?" Cara had always considered her sister a genius. And she'd known for a few years now that Gillian's business was growing in leaps and bounds.

"You let it boggle your mind when you're in a room with the president?"

"Yes," Cara answered honestly.

"But not enough to stop you from doing your job."

"I suppose."

Gillian opened a recessed compartment next to her seat, extracting a bottle of water from a bed of ice cubes. "Why are we talking about this?"

"Because we're sitting in a ridiculously expensive jet, being pampered beyond what is reasonable."

Gillian buckled up, then gestured to the small trapdoor next to Cara's seat. "Thirsty?"

"Not really."

Cara tightened the seat belt across her hips. The jet began to taxi, turning on a dime to head for the runway.

Gillian unscrewed the cap on her bottle. "We should be talking about Max."

"I don't want to talk about Max." Cara changed her mind about the water, lifting the small, wood-grained lid of her seat compartment and taking a bottle.

Gillian leaned back against the headrest of her seat. "Was that a thump I heard in the middle of the night?"

"You mean the avalanche?"

"You falling off the wagon."

"Wagon?" Cara took a drink of the chilled water.

"The no-Max-Gray wagon."

Cara choked, struggling not to spit out the mouthful of water.

Gillian laughed at her struggle. "I'll take that as a yes."

"You should take it as shock," Cara wheezed. "At the audacity of your question."

Gillian waved a dismissive hand as the engines whined to full power. "But you did it, didn't you?"

"Yes," Cara admitted. "I did. Thanks to you. And I really don't want to talk about it."

"Why not?"

"Because I'm trying not to think about it."

"Is it working?"

"Not particularly."

Gillian's voice lowered, her expression going softer. "Sorry I left you."

"Why *did* you leave me?"

Gillian had been fully aware that Cara was fighting her feelings for Max. Leaving them alone together hadn't been a particularly supportive move.

"I was hungry," Gillian sheepishly admitted. "Jake seemed like a decent guy. I didn't expect the conference call. And I sure didn't expect an avalanche."

"You thought you'd be back before Max could seduce me?"

"I did. I didn't count on the two of you rushing for the bedroom the minute we cleared the driveway."

"That's *not* how it happened."

"No kidding."

"I held out for a while. But he practically saved my life. I mean, well, he would probably have saved my life. If the avalanche had hit the villa and the roof had caved in." Cara's memory went back to those few moments when she'd thought they might die, the feel of Max's body sheltering her, his strength, his ingenuity.

The jet sped its way along the frozen asphalt, lifting smoothly into the air before banking around the mountain peaks.

"How did it happen?" asked Gillian.

Cara frowned at the question. "I think you want us to be closer than sisters ought to be."

"We've always been closer than sisters ought to be."

It was true. "You want to know which position we used and what he whispered in my ear?"

Gillian answered with a broad grin. "I want to know what you were thinking the moment before you said yes and took off your clothes."

"I was thinking no, no, no, no, *no*."

"Clearly, that worked."

"I was making a reasoned and logical argument inside my head for keeping my hands completely to myself."

"And?"

"And he told me I was overthinking."

"Were you?"

"I'm always overthinking. There's nothing wrong with overthinking. You generally come to much better decisions when you're overthinking."

"So what happened?" Gillian prompted.

"He kissed me."

"Just up and kissed you?"

"Just up and kissed me. He didn't have a counterargument. There wasn't a single point for his side."

"So he kissed you instead."

Cara felt a little shiver at the memory. "And that was all she wrote. Next thing I knew, I was naked."

Gillian laughed. "I'm sorry. I know it's not funny. But I love that my coolly logical, self-contained, controlled sister got swept away by inappropriate passion."

Cara sent her a glare. "Well, I didn't love it at all," she lied.

"Was it bad?" asked Gillian, sobering.

"No." Cara couldn't bring herself to lie about that.

"Good?"

"So good," Cara swallowed. Forget the top ten, Max had to be the hottest man alive, and heaven had to be just like those moments in his arms.

"So what now?"

"Nothing now. It's done. It's over."

"You broke up with him?"

"There was nothing to break. We were never together. But I made him promise that he'd stay away from me. He has principles. He'll keep his word."

Gillian was silent for a long moment. "You think that was smart?"

"It was brilliant." Cara trusted Max more than she trusted herself.

"I guess that's one problem solved." As the plane leveled off, Gillian unbuckled her seat belt. "But what will you do when your pregnancy starts showing? D.C.'s a pretty small town. Max is going to hear that you're pregnant."

"I have a plan," said Cara, shifting to get comfortable in her seat, telling herself it was past time to stop talking and thinking about Max. It was her and the baby from here on in.

"Oh, do tell," Gillian encouraged.

"I'm requesting a transfer to one of our foreign embassies. Maybe Australia, maybe Canada or England. There are plenty of places for me to go." She made a show of glancing around the plane's interior. "And it's not like you can't come and visit whenever you want."

"Would they give you a transfer?"

"I hope so. Maybe. I think I have a good chance."

"And, if they don't?"

"They will."

"Cara—"

"I don't need plan C, D and F."

Gillian opened her mouth, but Cara didn't let her get in a word. "I'm not you," said Cara.

"And I'm not pregnant," Gillian retorted.

"Really? You're going to go there?"

"I'm just sayin', you were probably hoping the birth control would work, too."

"What made you so mean?"

"If your big sister won't tell you the truth, who will?"

"That's not the truth. That's your paranoid view of the world."

"If we don't break into the India market," Gillian said reasonably, "we'll try for Brazil."

"So, you'll still become a billionaire."

"Exactly."

"And that was a metaphor for good contingency planning?"

"It was. You can't do these things on the fly. I already have staff in South America. We've got a dozen in-market consultants working from Chile to Colombia. But, for your circumstances, good contingency planning says you need to let Max know the two of you weren't exclusive. And you need to do it now, before any hint or whisper of pregnancy comes up."

"Just call him up?" Cara challenged, knowing it was ridiculous. She could never pull that off. Not with Max. Maybe not with anyone.

"You could be a little more subtle than that."

"He'd know I was lying."

"How would he know?"

"Because I could never do it with a straight face."

"Really?"

"Yes, really."

"Hmm." Gillian went silent for a moment. "Okay, then I'll do it for you."

Cara scoffed. "I think we're above and beyond sisterhood again."

"I'd do anything for you."

Cara cocked her head and cast her sister a baleful look. "You'll tell Max that I've been sleeping with other men?"

"Please. Give me a little credit. I won't tell Max. I'll tell Jake."

Cara gave a slow blink of astonishment. "Jake?"

"He liked me," said Gillian. "Or at least he was attracted to me. He was definitely flirting with me."

Cara had no doubt it was true. "You don't think it'll look suspicious if you call him up to talk about my sex life?" The idea was so preposterous, she didn't know whether to laugh or shriek.

"He'll call me."

"What? When? Wait a minute. Did you sleep with Jake?"

"No," Gillian huffed. "I did not sleep with Jake. I only just met the man."

"But he stayed in your hotel suite last night."

"Where else was he going to stay? The hotels were completely full, and his villa was hit by an avalanche."

Cara quirked a meaningful eyebrow.

"Listen, missy." Gillian wagged her finger in mock admonishment. "It was a big suite, and I behaved myself."

"Did you like him?" Cara asked, contemplating the possibilities.

"I don't know. I suppose." Gillian's gaze moved to the window. "He's kinda cute and funny. He's got a wicked sense of irony. You know, it's been a long time since any guy completely ignored my money."

"He didn't notice the three-thousand-dollar-a-night hotel suite?"

"If he did, he didn't say much. But back to you. All I have to do is mention to Jake that I'm in D.C. He'll talk me into a drink and voilà."

"Voilà? In between martinis, you bring up your sister's sex life?"

"Easy, peasy."

"No," Cara told her with conviction.

"You don't have to lift a finger."

"No."

Gillian looked carefully into her eyes. "You sure?"

"I'm positive." She was. Sort of. Maybe.

She couldn't deny the utility of Max thinking someone else was the father. But she wasn't ready to let him think she'd betrayed him.

Then again, maybe *betrayal* was too strong a word. They'd dated casually, never had an understanding of any kind. Maybe he already thought she'd been with other men. Maybe he'd been with other woman.

She swallowed. She knew it wasn't her right to care. But she cared very much.

* * *

"Your instincts are second to none." Max's former boss, Marnie Salloway, hit the remote, shutting off the video segment from the Fields avalanche. Max hadn't worked with the woman in years, not since she was an associate producer and he was fresh out of college at in Maryland. But he'd answered her summons for a meeting. He wanted to look her in the eyes and ask a few questions.

"Right place, right time," said Max, turning in his chair at the long, oval table in the office boardroom.

"Juxtaposed with the snowboard lessons, you look like the all-American guy."

"Hardly," Max scoffed.

Marnie gave him a knowing smile. "And you look so darn good doing it."

"Are you flirting with me?"

She was at least ten years older than Max. He'd been the object of her attention in the past, and he had no wish to repeat the experience. He also hoped to throw her off her game. If Liam Fisher was right and ANS was playing fast and loose with the law in getting their info on the Ariella Winthrop scandal, Marnie would be in the thick of it.

"Absolutely not," she trilled. "Please. I'm merely saying what we both know. You're a star, Max. Though now that we're talking about it, I think you've gone just about as far as you can go over at NCN. When are you going to consider joining a real network?"

"NCN feels pretty real to me."

"Not according to the latest ratings. Well, your show is doing fine."

"Which would be my primary concern."

Marnie sat forward, her fire-engine-red nails clashing with her rather orange-hued hair. "I'm not talking about how your show is doing now. I'm talking about what you could be doing from here. Our budget is higher. We have more viewers. And

we'd be willing to look at giving you some producer respon-
sibilities. Think about it, Max. You could influence the direction of your stories and your show."

"I'm happy with my show's budget and direction."

She cocked her head, showing a brittle, knowing smile.
"You need me to sweeten the pot?"

Max didn't respond, curious where she was going and how
much she might divulge.

"I have a drawer full of stories, juicy stories, stories that
nobody else even knows are out there."

"Tell me more," he encouraged. "What does ANS have that
others don't?"

"Superior investigative skills."

"Did you use them on the Ariella Winthrop story, Marnie?
How exactly did you get that?"

Suspicion came into her blue eyes.

"How do I know you can get more?" he persisted, trying to
throw her off his main purpose.

She was obviously hesitant. "Are you telling me you're ready
to jump ship?"

"I'm willing to think about it. How'd you do it?"

"Right place, right time," she told him softly.

But it was triumph he saw in her eyes, pride and triumph.
He'd bet a whole lot of money that ANS had done something
underhanded and that Marnie was behind it.

He gazed levelly across the table. "Anybody can get lucky
once."

"ANS gets lucky a whole lot more than once."

"And I'd be able to take advantage of that luck?"

"Absolutely."

After a silent moment, Max realized he wasn't going to get
anything more here today. "Can I have a few days to think
about it?"

The caution was back in her expression. "Don't take too
long."

He rose from his chair. "Thanks for inviting me to the meeting, Marnie."

She rose with him. "Thanks for thinking of ANS."

"You're all I've been thinking about."

She smiled at that, and he was positive she didn't understand the irony. Thank goodness. It had been a stupid, self-indulgent thing for him to say.

He left the boardroom, took the elevator to the lobby and exited onto the street. Jake was waiting two blocks down, around the corner at Rene's Café.

As Max took the concrete stairs to sidewalk level, his phone chimed. It was his boss at NCN, producer Nadine Clarke.

"Hey," he greeted. The sounds of the busy production office echoed in the background.

"What's this I hear about you meeting with Marnie Salloway?"

"Are you kidding me?" Max glanced behind him at the office building. "That was barely three minutes ago."

"What can I say? We're a news network. People love to leak to me."

"I'm impressed," said Max, stopping for the light.

It was late afternoon, and the sun was setting behind the downtown office buildings. A few flakes of snow wafted down, making an already cold evening feel colder.

"Do I have something to worry about?" asked Nadine.

"Not a thing."

"Good." Her tone was crisp and no-nonsense. "I need you to pack for L.A. The president's leaving for the Pacific Rim Economic Summit in a couple of days, and I need you to stay on the story. We're going to do a remote episode from L.A., haven't figured out the details yet."

"I wanted to talk to you about that," said Max, navigating around a taxi as he moved with the crowd across the street. "I'm not sure the president is the real story here."

"Really?" Nadine drawled in a tone Max recognized. The

woman had already made up her mind and wasn't interested in hearing anything that conflicted with her own view.

He persevered, "I think we should figure out how ANS discovered the story."

"And I think we should figure out how NCN finishes the story. And since I'm the producer, let's try it my way, shall we?"

"Do you even want to know why?" Max pressed.

"Max, you already talked me into hiring Liam. I assume he's going to eventually tell us why."

"Liam needs some help."

"He's doing fine for the moment. But you can tell me more when you get back from L.A."

"Yes, boss," Max drawled.

"That's what I like to hear." Then there was a slight pause. "Unless, of course, you truly are considering an offer from ANS. In which case, let's do dinner so I can massage your ego for a while and offer you a raise."

"Not necessary."

"Good. Your flight leaves at nine." Nadine rang off.

Phone to her left ear, Lynn waved Cara into her office.

"Without any new facts, it's hard to keep them from speculating," Lynn said into the phone.

Cara's coworker Sandy followed her into the office and set a stack of papers on the corner of Lynn's desk.

"*The Morning News,*" said Sandy. "*The Night Show, D.C. Beat* and *Hello Virginia.* They all want the president."

Lynn covered the mouthpiece. "Nobody's getting the president."

"*Hello Virginia* promised to be nice and let him tell his side of the story."

"No, Barry," Lynn said into the phone to the chief of staff. She clenched her jaw for a moment. "Because I don't have magical powers. I don't. No." She shook the telephone receiver dramatically in front of her before putting it back to her ear. "You do that. Tell me what he says." She slammed down the phone.

"Like hell they'll let him tell his side of the story," she said to Sandy, her hand going to her ring.

Cara agreed with her boss. The second *Hello Virginia* got the president in front of a microphone, they'd hit him with every awkward question possible.

Lynn twisted her topaz ring. "We need you on the trip, Cara."

"Which trip?" Cara asked, taking a seat.

"The Pacific Rim Economic Summit. L.A."

Cara was surprised. It was a plum assignment. "You're not going?"

She caught Sandy's annoyed glance as the woman left the room, but forced herself to dismiss it. If it was professional jealousy, Sandy would just have to deal with it. Barry and Lynn set the agenda, nobody else.

"I'm not going," Lynn confirmed. "Barry wants me here. And he was impressed by the way you handled the fallout at the inaugural ball."

"I was just doing what you taught me." Cara wasn't flattering her boss. She was honestly in awe of Lynn's skill at spin. The woman might be a bit prickly, but she was also brilliant.

"Well, you caught Barry's attention, and the president heard how well you did."

Cara slumped back in her chair. "Really?"

"Yes."

"Really?"

"Don't act so shocked." Lynn turned to her keyboard and typed a few words. "You'll need to head for L.A. a couple of days early. Tomorrow would be best. Security and the advance team are already there."

Cara sat up straight. "You bet."

"I'm emailing you the events list. His speeches are in editing, but we'll want some additional speaking points in anticipation of ad hoc questions. Barry will try to keep him away from the press, but somebody might shove a microphone in front of his face on a red carpet somewhere."

"Will do." Cara jotted down a few notes to herself.

"So you'll be handling most of the informal questions."

Cara jerked her head up. "Huh?"

"We can't give them the president."

"But—"

"You'll be fine," Lynn reassured her.

"I haven't done anything unscripted for the president." Cara was nowhere near ready for that.

"What do you call the inaugural ball?"

"An emergency."

"And you stepped up to the plate."

Cara swallowed. "I'm, uh, flattered, of course."

Lynn's expression turned serious. "This is a golden opportunity, Cara."

"What if I blow it?"

"Would I set you up to fail?"

At Cara's hesitation, Lynn answered her own question. "I would not."

"Not intentionally," Cara allowed.

"Are you questioning my judgment?"

"No, no, of course not."

"Good. The president wants you in L.A. Barry has faith in you. And so do I. Don't psych yourself out."

"I won't," Cara vowed. She rose to her feet.

"Go pack your evening gowns. There'll be some parties."

Eight

It was unseasonably warm in L.A., especially for January. It was barely 7:00 a.m., but Cara was hot jogging along the beach path at the Santa Monica shore. She stripped off her sweatshirt and tied it around her waist, letting her bare arms drink in the cool breeze coming off the ocean. She'd been sweating against her tank top, and the cooling dampness reenergized her pace.

The waves foamed rhythmically against the sand, while early traffic wound its way along Ocean Avenue. The president's advance contingent was set up at the Jade Bay hotel, where the high-level trade meetings would take place. The president was due to attend three luncheons, two dinners and a final reception following a formal joint statement from the participants on the results of the summit.

Cara's cell phone chimed on her hip, and she extracted it from its case. It wasn't a number she recognized.

"Yeah?" she breathed.

"Cara?"

"Ari—" She stopped herself from saying Ariella's full name.

"It's me," Ariella responded.

"Are you okay? Where are you? No. Wait. Don't answer that."

"I'm in Seattle."

As she approached the pier, Cara slowed to a walk. "I told you not to answer."

Ariella's voice turned wistful. "I'm not staying here much longer. I thought it would be more remote. You know, trees and mountains, maybe a log cabin by a stream."

Having visited her sister in Seattle, Cara couldn't help but smile.

"It's huge," said Ariella. "And there are so many people."

"Over half a million," said Cara. "Is everything okay?"

"I'm getting scared."

"Of what?"

"Of being found out, of being recognized. I'm staying in the hotel as much as possible, but when I go out, people look at me like they know me, but they can't quite place me."

"I guess you've seen the TV reports," said Cara.

"I have. It's bad, isn't it?"

"The opposition is calling for the president's resignation. But they do that at the drop of a hat. What's worse is that he's been steadily dropping in the polls."

"I'm not helping, am I?"

"None of this is your fault."

"But I want to help," said Ariella. "I admire the president. You know how much I respect him."

"I do."

"What can I do?"

"Do you want me to answer that question as the president's public relations specialist or your friend?"

"What can I do to help the president?"

Cara drew a deep sigh, raking back her damp hair and plunking down on a bench beneath a palm tree. "Take the DNA test."

Ariella went silent for a moment. "I guess I knew that was going to be your answer."

"It's what's best for the president. I'll be honest with you, we need to move on from the uncertainty. Whatever the outcome, we can spin it a number of ways. Ironically, either answer would make it less newsworthy."

"I understand."

"I'm sorry," Cara said softly.

Ariella gave a light laugh. "It's not your fault, either. Anything else?"

"What do you mean?"

"Is there anything else I can do? I thought hiding out was the best move. But I realize it was the selfish move. I left all of you behind to face the music."

"It's what I'm paid for," Cara pointed out.

"What about that guy?"

Cara didn't understand. "There's a guy?"

"Max Gray. He helped me get away the night after the ball."

Cara's stomach lurched in response to Max's name. "I heard about that," was all she said.

"All the stations keep running the same footage over and over, the president looking shocked when that horrible Mitch person made the toast. I was thinking that if I went on Max's show and made a new statement, gave them something fresh, it would take some of the heat off the president."

"That's not a good idea, Ariella." Max and NCN, like any news organization, couldn't be trusted to act in the best interest of anything but their story.

"You're talking as my friend, aren't you?" Ariella asked.

It was true. Cara was speaking as a friend.

"You should turn into the president's public relations specialist for a minute."

"Ariella."

"I'm asking the public relations specialist. Would it help if I went on Max's show?"

"It would be dangerous. It could go either way."

"I trust Max."

"I don't." Right now, Cara couldn't afford to trust a single member of the press.

"Talk to Lynn," Ariella encouraged her. "See what she thinks I should do."

Cara knew she had to do exactly that. She wouldn't be doing her job if she didn't bring this opportunity to her boss's attention. But she also feared she knew what Lynn would say to the offer. She'd take it in a heartbeat.

"I will," Cara promised. "And I'm also calling my sister. She's in Seattle, and she can help you while you're there."

"I won't be here much longer."

"Gillian can help. Her house is huge and secluded, and she has security."

"Okay," Ariella agreed, a trace of relief in her voice.

Cara ended the call and came to her feet. The Jade Bay hotel was directly across the street, and she needed a secure line for the conversation with Lynn.

When Max's phone rang, he was deep in Malibu Creek State Park, racing Jake downhill on a mountain bike, coming around a tight switchback, avoiding the rocks and scrub brush while ducking beneath an overhanging tree. He splashed through the creek to a wide, grassy spot and skidded his back tire to a stop, cursing out loud.

Jake slammed on his own brakes, but he passed Max before pivoting his bike and sliding to a stop.

"What?" he demanded.

Max ripped off his helmet, fishing into a pocket of his khakis for the phone. He held it up to show Jake, who rolled his own eyes as he removed his helmet.

"Nadine," Max told Jake.

"Impeccable timing, as always," Jake responded, dismounting to lay his bike on its side.

"Hey, Nadine," Max greeted a little breathlessly, following Jake's lead and leaning his own bike down on the grassy patch.

"Have I got a show for you." There was no mistaking the excitement in Nadine's voice.

"Good to hear," Max responded. Whatever it was, he was glad Nadine was happy. When she was happy, everyone was happy. He bent to retrieve his water bottle from the rack on the bike frame, popping the top.

"I just got off the phone with Lynn Larson."

Max stopped. "You got the president for my show?"

"No, no. Not the president. You think I have superpowers? And what's the matter with you, anyway? Everything's going to be anticlimactic after that guess."

"Sorry," said Max.

Nadine harrumphed at the other end.

"Tell me about it," Max prompted. "I promise to be excited." He squirted a stream of water into his dry mouth. The scenery in the park was fantastic, but the dust was pervasive, and, as usual, Jake set a harsh pace.

"Oh, you will be excited," said Nadine. "I got Ariella."

"Ariella Winthrop?" Max raised his brows in Jake's direction.

Jake crossed his arms over his chest, obviously waiting for the conversation to continue.

"Yes, Ariella Winthrop," Nadine returned sarcastically. "Is there another Ariella in the world at the moment?"

Max ignored the rhetorical question. "I thought she'd left town."

"Well, she's coming back. Or, rather, she's coming there."

"To L.A.? You know this how?"

"Lynn Larson. Didn't I just say that?"

"I don't understand," said Max.

Judging by the expression on Jake's face, he was equally confused.

"I don't know what you did, Max. But Ariella herself requested your show. They have some restrictions, of course. But nothing we can't live with. It'll be a short segment, but what a coup. And Caroline Cranshaw will be there."

Max stomach contracted. "Cara?"

Nadine didn't seem to hear him. "I assume Caroline will be the handler, so we don't get too much out of Ariella, but—"

"Cara Cranshaw, from the White House, has agreed to come on my show?" Max locked gazes with Jake.

Jake now knew all about Max's relationship with Cara. After what had happened in Fields, it seemed much safer to have Jake working with them, rather than getting curious.

"She's already in L.A. with the advance team. Lynn's going to call and let her know, and then we'll nail down the details."

It sounded like Cara didn't know about this yet. Max could only imagine how she was going to react.

"I'm just giving you a heads-up," said Nadine.

"I appreciate that."

"What time is it there?"

"Coming up on seven."

"It's ten here. I probably won't hear any more tonight. So, talk tomorrow."

"Talk tomorrow," Max parroted, then ended the call.

"You want to catch me up?" asked Jake.

"Why would Ariella surface?" Max mused to himself.

"I thought you were going to respect a certain perimeter when it came to Cara."

"I did, too." Max dropped the phone back into his pocket. "Her boss may not have talked to her yet. But we've got her and Ariella for the remote from Grauman's Chinese Theatre. It sounds like Cara's already in L.A."

"What about her sister?" asked Jake.

Max lifted his bike. "Forget about her sister. Gillian's smart, gorgeous and filthy rich. She can have any guy in the world."

"Hey, I'm a guy. I'm in the world. My odds are just as good anyone else's."

"No, they're not. The woman's got a master's degree from MIT. She hangs out with the who's who of international commerce. They have private jets, yachts moored in the South of France, hotel buildings and their own sous chefs."

Jake retrieved his own bike, tipping his chin in the air with mock indignation. "I don't like to throw this around a lot. But I'm a graduate of the Stony Hills Digital Film Academy."

"I've seen your résumé," Max drawled. "I've also seen your apartment, and I know your net worth. Forget Gillian. Go back to Jessica."

Jake remounted. "Jessica's history. I've been told I'm good in bed."

Max balanced one foot on a pedal. "By women you were paying to be there?"

"Well, if you're gonna get all picky about it."

Max grinned. "How many miles to the parking lot?"

"Seven," said Jake, cinching up his helmet. "And then, buddy, is it ever Miller time."

"The Jade Bay hotel lounge?"

Jake chuckled. "You've got it bad."

"I want to see what I'm up against."

"Really?" Jake asked. "You're going to give me that kind of an opening?"

"Get stuffed," said Max, rolling his bike toward an incline.

"You're up against Cara," Jake called out from behind. "At least you were at one time. Not so much anymore."

Max poured on the power on his way up the hill, wishing his pulse would pound the memories out of his mind. Keeping his promise to Cara was enough of a battle while she was on the other side of the country. Working with her on a show was going to make it impossible.

Feeling irritated and determined, Cara spotted Max from across the patio lounge of the hotel. The night was cool, propane heaters humming between tables, steam wafting from the pools that were lit underwater with red, blue and green lights. Tiny white lights twinkled in the trees, while men in suits and women in cocktail dresses enjoyed an evening drink among the dining tables, the deeply padded loungers and the private cabanas.

Max was sitting at the bar, his back to her, and the seats on either side of him were empty. His shirt was white, sleeves rolled up to the middle of his forearms. He wore black slacks and casual shoes. A tall, elegant glass of amber beer sat on the bar in front of him.

Cara was returning from a dinner meeting with her White House colleagues in a private room on the top floor of a neighboring hotel. Lynn's direction had been clear: NCN wanted Ariella, and they wanted Cara. And the White House was going to take advantage of the opportunity.

Careful of her dignity in her little black dress, Cara shimmied up onto the bar stool beside Max, hooking her four-inch heels on the crossbar of the high chair.

"Is this your idea of a loophole?" she asked without preamble. "Getting me assigned to your show?"

Max half turned, showing no surprise at seeing her in Los Angeles. "It wasn't my idea."

"I'm sure," she drawled.

The bartender appeared in front of her.

"Orange juice, please."

"Your boss called my boss and offered up Ariella. What were we supposed to do?"

"And you added me in the bargain," Cara accused, reaching for an almond from the small dish on the bar. Though she'd just eaten a chicken breast, stir-fried garden vegetables and rice pilaf, she was ridiculously hungry.

Max swiveled to face her head on. "When I want you, Cara, I'll come after you. I'm not going to sneak around behind your back."

"I don't believe you." This had to be more than a coincidence.

"Don't you?" he asked softly.

She couldn't bring herself to answer. As far as she knew, he'd never lied to her before. And he looked sincere now.

"We can't do this, Max." There was a husky tremor to her voice. She hadn't realized until this moment how much she missed him. Life had been colorless since they'd parted. Sitting this close, it was a struggle to keep from reaching for him, touching his hair, stroking his cheek, pressing her lips to his.

"We're professionals," he countered, green eyes darkening, as if he was reading her mind.

For a moment, she forgot to breathe.

The waiter set a tall glass of orange juice on the bar.

"Hey, Cara." Jake's voice broke the moment.

She gave herself a mental shake, raising her gaze as Jake eased into the seat on the opposite side of Max.

"Hi, Jake. I didn't know you were here."

Jake scooped up a handful of the almonds. "I don't dare stay far away from this guy. Stories have a way of finding him."

She couldn't disagree with that. Max was three thousand miles from D.C., and Ariella was about to be plunked in his lap.

"I hear NCN is getting a scoop," she said to Jake.

He grinned in return. "How's your sister?"

Max shot Jake a dark look.

"What?" Jake asked with mock innocence.

"Can we keep Gillian out of this?" asked Max.

"She's fine," said Cara, thinking her sister had obviously been right about Jake's interest. No huge surprise there.

Jake dumped the remainder of the almonds into his palm. "Had dinner?" he asked Cara.

It was on the tip of her tongue to admit she had, but her stomach rumbled beneath the black dress. "I could eat," she admitted.

Jake came to his feet. "Let's grab a table."

"You are not going to use dinner as an excuse to grill her for information," Max warned.

"Gillian's on her way here," said Cara, tucking her tiny black evening purse under her arm.

Jake pulled up short. "Hello?"

Even Max looked interested by that.

"She's flying Ariella down from Seattle in her jet."

Gillian had made the decision to come to L.A. the second she'd heard Max was in town and that Cara was going to be forced to do a show with him. Cara tried to tell her she didn't need hand-holding. But Gillian had insisted she did. And maybe Gillian was right. It would be good to have her here.

"Seattle," Max mused under his breath. "Not a bad place to hide."

"When's she getting here?" asked Jake.

Max shook his head at Jake. He motioned to a passing waiter and asked for a table.

"Tomorrow night," Cara answered Jake, falling into step behind Max as they wended their way across the patio.

Jake walked beside her. "Moral support?" he asked.

Cara shot him a curious look. "What do you mean?"

"I know about you and Max."

Cara was struck speechless.

"Trying to keep your hands off each other," Jake finished.

"What?" she managed to choke out.

Max came to a halt beside a round table, turning and pulling out a chair for Cara.

"You *told* him?" she demanded, refusing to sit down.

The waiter glanced from one to the other and smoothly withdrew.

"I can be trusted," Jake put in.

"We're better off with him covering for us than snooping around."

"You swore you wouldn't tell anyone."

"Did you tell Gillian?"

"Yes, but…" That was different. Gillian was her sister. She was intensely loyal, and she'd never do anything to harm Cara.

Max lifted a brow.

"That's different," she finished.

"How?" he asked reasonably.

Wasn't it obvious? "She's my sister."

"I've put my life in Jake's hands more than once," said Max.

"And I've put my life in his," said Jake.

Cara turned to look at Jake. Despite her anger, she regretted that she was put in the position of insulting him. He'd always struck her as a perfectly decent guy, and none of this was his fault. But the only way to keep secrets was to hold them close.

"I've got your back," he told her, sincerity in the depths of his gray eyes. "You should sit down and have something to eat."

Something told Cara to trust him. Max obviously did. She wasn't happy about Max sharing, but she had to believe Jake wouldn't betray Max.

She sat down in the padded rattan chair.

A split second later, the waiter reappeared, placing a white linen napkin in her lap with a flourish.

Max and Jake took the chairs on either side of her.

"Wine?" asked Max, reaching for the dark green, leather-bound list.

Just then, another waiter arrived with the drinks they'd left at the bar, setting them on the table.

"I think I'll stick with the juice," she answered, lifting the glass and taking a sip.

"Afraid of losing control around me?" he teased.

"Yes."

Her answer seemed to throw him, and their gazes locked.

Jake glanced from one to the other, his voice going low as he bent across the table. "Just so I'm clear. Do you want me to cover up what happened in Montana, or do you need me to stop it from happening again while we're here?"

"We're fine," said Max, but just then his knee brushed

Cara's. An electric current ran the length of her thigh, settling at the apex, causing her muscles to contract. She knew she had to draw away, break the connection, but she was powerless to do it.

"You sure?" Jake drawled. "Because I'm available for, you know, standing guard at hotel room doors or hosing you down."

Max turned to frown at his friend.

Jake gave an unrepentant grin. "Unless, of course, I make some headway with Gillian. In that case, you two are on your own."

"Let's talk about the show," said Max. His tone turned crisp, but his eyes were still warm when they returned to Cara, and he kept his knee pressed up against hers.

"Sure," she squeaked, earning a curious glance from Jake.

"We've been told we have two minutes with Ariella. It'll be pretaped, three scripted questions, no deviation."

"Can you tell us about your childhood?" Cara listed the questions Lynn had given to her. "Do you know anything about your birth parents? And did you ever have reason to suspect President Morrow might be your father?"

"I can live with those," said Max.

"I'll be there to make sure you don't deviate." She'd seen enough of Max's work to know he'd try to catch Ariella off guard by chatting casually, then create some B-roll footage to exploit later.

"I'll behave," Max vowed, but something in his tone made her nervous.

Max shifted, and Cara was quickly reminded that he was still touching her. How had she forgotten?

"I'll also need to see the edited version."

"Nadine agreed to that?" Max sounded skeptical.

"I guess Lynn can outnegotiate Nadine."

Jake laughed. "Wow. Then I'd hate to be across the table from Lynn."

"She's a force of nature," said Cara.

"You can't fight nature," Max told her in a soft voice.

She tried to pull away from his touch, but her limbs weren't cooperating. He was pressed more fully against her now, and her body was absorbing little pulses of sensation.

"Am I missing something?" asked Jake, taking in their expressions.

"Nothing," said Max, but he didn't back off. "Nadine also wants a few minutes on the summit and a couple of clips of the president," he told Cara. "What's he going to be talking about here?"

"Energy." She struggled to keep her voice even. "Natural gas. And technology, aerospace and aviation in particular. They're a big deal under the free trade talks."

"Manning Aviation?" Max asked Jake. "We can probably get something on the Stram-4000 prototype."

Just then, the waiter arrived, setting a gold-embossed, leather-bound menu in front of each of them.

"You should be talking to Gillian," Cara put in without thinking.

Jake instantly glanced up.

"She's working on a technology deal with China and another one with India. She has exactly the kind of company that will benefit from these trade negotiations."

Max and Jake exchanged a look.

"Would she do it?" asked Max.

"Is her deal confidential?" asked Jake.

Cara hadn't thought about that. "We'd have to ask her."

"I'll do that," Jake quickly volunteered. "I can pick her up at the airport." Then he smirked. "But you two have to promise to behave while I'm gone."

Cara couldn't help stealing a glance at Max.

He was looking straight back, his eyes smoldering with obvious desire. She felt the impact right down to her toes.

Nine

"Do you think it's fate?" Gillian called from the bedroom of her suite at the Jade Bay hotel.

"I think it's karma," Cara replied, moving from the dining room to the butler's pantry, then peeking into the powder room. "Clearly I did something terrible in a past life. Why do you get such huge hotel rooms?"

Gillian was on the eighty-first floor, with a panoramic view of the Santa Monica Pier. Cara was down on ten, with a view of the lobby roof and the financial building across the street.

Gillian emerged through the double doors of the bedroom. "I don't book them myself. I think we have a travel person who does that. And you couldn't have done anything bad in a past life. You're an incredibly good person."

"Then why is Max in L.A.? Why did Ariella offer to do his show? And why did I open my big mouth and tell them you had a deal with China?"

"It'll be publicity for me," said Gillian. "That never hurts."

"So, clearly, you were very good in a past life."

Gillian grinned at that.

"They want to film your interview at the Manning Aviation facility. Their jet prototype has a technology angle."

"Being pregnant's not a cosmic punishment, you know," Gillian pointed out.

Cara wandered to the wet bar, checking out the liquor selection and the complimentary hors d'oeuvres and glancing at the dozens of crystal glasses in assorted shapes and sizes. "The situation feels like a punishment."

"You should tell him."

Cara shook her head.

"He might surprise you."

"He's not going to surprise me." Cara prided herself on being honest and practical.

Gillian moved across the room. "He's going to know eventually." She put her hand gently on Cara's stomach. "This little guy or girl is not going to stay hidden forever."

"I have a while yet."

"If you're not going to tell him, then you need to get some distance from Max."

Cara gave a pained laugh. "I came all the way across the country."

"Not that kind of distance. Maybe find yourself a new boyfriend. Make it obvious you're dating someone else."

"And bring them in on a conspiracy?" Cara couldn't see that working.

"Max needs to think it's not his baby."

"Yeah, I know he does," Cara admitted softly.

But for the moment, Cara needed to stop dwelling on her problems. She twisted open a bottle of imported water and helped herself to a savory pastry. "Dear sister, have you actually gotten used to all this luxury?"

It was Gillian's turn to glance around the massive suite. "I usually end up hosting business meetings and impromptu receptions. So having the big table is a plus."

"We could throw one heck of a party here," Cara noted.

The living and dining areas could fit thirty or forty people; add to that the huge deck, and the number probably went up to seventy. The dining table alone sat fourteen. The master suite was twice the size of Cara's hotel room.

"You want to have a party?" Gillian asked.

Cara shook her head. "The president arrives tomorrow, and I've got two formal dinners in a row. And I'm so tired lately. By ten, I'm ready to fall into bed. And hungry. I swear I could eat five meals a day."

"You should be eating well."

"I'm definitely eating very well. But I will be happy to get home to my own bed."

"I got Ariella set up with a lab in D.C.," said Gillian, changing the topic. "She's heading home after the show to take the DNA test."

Cara had seen Ariella briefly when they had arrived at the hotel. But Gillian had arranged for private security, who'd whisked her up to her own room right away.

"How's she doing?" Cara asked softly.

Gillian moved to one of the comfy sofa groupings. "Ariella's fine. Better than I expected. You're the one I'm worried about. The more I think about it, the more I realize it's not good for you to be around Max."

"It would be better if he wasn't here," Cara readily agreed, sinking down into a cream-colored armchair. "It all just feels so complicated. I know what I'm supposed to do. I know how I'm supposed to feel."

Gillian sat down across from her. "But you don't?"

"He's so...I don't know. I mean, I'm not supposed to want him. I shouldn't even like him, because he's so obstinate and sarcastic. But he's smart, Gilly. He's funny. And every time he touches me, my entire body lights up."

Gillian sat forward. "He's been touching you?"

"Not like that. Inadvertently, little brushes, things like that."

"They're on purpose," Gillian told her with authority.

"I know they're on purpose," Cara admitted. "And I don't pull away. It's a little game."

"I know that little game. It's called playing with fire."

Cara couldn't help a reflexive grin. "Do you think that's what makes it so sexy? That it's illicit and clandestine?"

"Illicit and clandestine always makes things sexy."

"So, maybe it's not just Max. Maybe I'd feel this way about any guy who was off-limits."

"Maybe." But Gillian looked doubtful. Then she paused, seeming to choose her words. "Cara, is there any chance you've fallen in love with him?"

Cara's stomach caved in on itself. "No," she insisted with a shake of her head. "No. It's not that."

It couldn't be that. Falling in love with Max would be a colossal mistake. And, anyway, she hadn't known him nearly long enough to have fallen in love.

"I like him," she told Gillian. "But I don't love him. I mean, I admire some things about him. But on some fundamental levels, like how we feel about family and children, we're on two completely different planets."

"That's good," Gillian told her with conviction.

"It's great," Cara readily agreed. Maybe if she said it often enough, it would come true.

Since Cara knew Ariella so well, she could tell she was nervous on the stage of the theater. But to a casual onlooker, Ari would only look poised and beautiful. Max sat in the opposite armchair, and the two were surrounded by a jumble of cameras, cables, lights and bustling crew members.

Cara stood off to one side, her heart going out to Ariella. She was incredibly brave to do this for the president.

Finally, it got quiet. The director gave a signal, and everyone stepped out of the shot. The sound and camera crews confirmed their readiness, and Max sat straight in his chair, putting on his formal interviewer's expression.

"We're here in L.A. with Ariella Winthrop, who has been in hiding since news broke of her possible link to President Morrow."

Cara wasn't crazy about the in-hiding reference, but it wasn't enough to shut it down.

"Ariella, welcome to the show." Max turned on the charm. "We all know you were adopted. Can you tell us about your childhood with Berry and Frank Winthrop?"

"Thank you, Max. I'm pleased to be here. The Winthrops were wonderful parents. They raised me in Chester, Montana. My father was very involved in the community. He coached my softball team." She gave what looked like a fond, wistful smile. "I wasn't a star player, but I loved spending Sundays with my father. My mother worked from home, so she was always there when I came home from school. She loved to bake. I kept her secret recipes, and they were the foundation of my current catering and event planning business."

"I understand your parents were killed in a light plane crash?"

Cara moved into Max's line of sight, giving him a warning glare for going off script.

But Ariella stepped up with aplomb.

"I miss them every day," she said. Then she stopped talking, leaving it to Max to fix the silence.

Cara smiled.

"Do you know anything about your birth parents?" Max asked.

Ariella shook her head. "I always knew I was adopted. My mother used to tell me they picked me because I was the best baby in the world. I understood the records were confidential, and I respected that. Many people have valid reasons for giving a baby up for adoption. And thank goodness they make that unselfish decision. I couldn't have asked for a better childhood, Max."

"Do you think the president lied about—"

"Stop the filming." Cara marched right into the camera shot, holding her hand in front of it, ensuring they wouldn't be able to use the question.

She glared at Max. "Stop it. Right now."

He held up his hands in surrender. "Sorry. Old habits die hard."

"Like hell," she muttered.

He grinned at her and pointed to his live mike.

"Don't do it again," she warned.

"I'm trying my best."

"Ms. Cranshaw," the director called out in obvious frustration. "Can you please get out of my camera shot?"

"Tell your interviewer to stick to the script."

"Stick to the script, Max," the director parroted without a trace of conviction.

Cara stepped back, staying poised and ready.

"Ariella," Max began again. "Before the inaugural ball, did you ever have reason to suspect President Morrow might be your father?"

"No reason at all, Max. I understand the American people are anxious to find out. But I have to say, I have the utmost respect for the president. I look at his positions on the economy, health care and international diplomacy, and I can't help but admire him. The voters made a great decision when they elected him, and I'm sure he will meet all of our expectations."

Ariella stopped speaking, and Cara all but cheered.

Max opened his mouth, but he caught Cara's warning glare and seemed to decide it wasn't worth it.

The director called a halt, and Ariella got to her feet.

Max stood. "Have you taken a DNA test?" he asked conversationally.

"Don't answer that." Cara quickly scooted in. "You're still wearing a microphone."

Ariella stood silently while the techs removed her mike and Max's.

"Can't blame a guy for trying," said Max.

"I can," Cara put in tartly.

"I'm sorry I couldn't help you more," Ariella said to Max.

"I hope you're doing okay," he responded, looking genuinely concerned.

"I'm—"

"Ariella," Cara warned. "He's not on our side."

"That's not strictly true," Max said to Cara, a rebuke in his tone.

"He seems like a good guy," Ariella told Cara. "You should really give him a chance."

Cara wished she could. But she didn't dare.

Max suspected Cara was keeping her distance from him at the Manning Aviation facility. She was far across the big hangar, chatting with a company vice president. The man was obviously taking advantage of having some face time with a member of the president's staff. The segment including the interview with Gillian had been taped and was finished. Most of the film crew had left, and Max and Jake were now checking out the new, single-engine planes being built at the facility.

They were ten passenger propeller planes, hot off the assembly line. They came with bush wheels, floats and skis. Both Max and Jake had private pilot licenses, and Max had been thinking about moving from his Cessna to something a little larger.

"Thought I'd try for another date with Gillian tonight," Jake was saying to Max while the Manning technician replaced the engine cover. Jake's gaze kept drifting to where Gillian was surrounded by half a dozen Manning employees, all men, all clearly vying for her attention.

"Looks like you've got some competition," Max observed.

"True enough." Jake seemed to hesitate. "Then again, there's competition everywhere," he stated, an odd note to his voice.

Max checked out his expression. "You mean for Gillian?"

"Gillian, Cara, any woman really."

Max's gaze flicked across the room. "I think that guy is more interested in President Morrow than in Cara." Not to mention that the vice president of Manning was at least sixty years old.

"Not him," said Jake.

"Then who?" Max drew back. "Not you."

"No, not me. But, you know, plenty of other guys probably find her attractive."

"Maybe," Max allowed.

He didn't really dwell on it, but he knew there had to be plenty of men interested in Cara. Maybe he didn't like to dwell on it because he didn't like the jolt of jealousy that invaded his gut when he did.

"You guys ever talk about stuff like that?" Jake asked, bending to check out the underside of the plane's tail.

"Talk about what?"

"Other guys." Jake ran his fingertips along the rounded edges.

"Why would we talk about other guys?" Apprehension prickled along Max's neck. "Where are you going with this?"

Jake straightened, expression tight. "Has Cara ever mentioned anyone else?"

"That she's dated?"

Had someone come out of the woodwork? From her past? Were they causing a problem? If that was the case, why didn't Jake just come straight-out and say it?

"What's going on?" Max demanded.

Jake glanced across the cavernous complex, then he seemed to check to be sure the technician was out of earshot. "Something Gillian said last night. It led me to believe you and Cara maybe weren't exclusive."

Everything inside Max went perfectly still and cold. "*What did Gillian say?*"

"I know the two of you are basically broken up, but what I don't understand is—"

"*What did Gillian say?*" Max had to stop himself from grabbing Jake by the collar.

"That you and Cara weren't exclusive."

"In those words."

Jake nodded. "In those words. I thought it was odd. I mean, you said you two have always kept it casual. But I thought that was because of your jobs. Cara never struck me as the kind of woman to have more than one lover." Jake glanced furtively away from Max's expression. "Not that it's any of my business. But I thought you should know."

Anger roiling, Max pivoted to glare across the hangar. He knew Cara was over there, but he couldn't focus on her through the red haze forming in front of his eyes.

His hands clenched into fists by his side. "Did Gillian mention a name?"

"Uh, Max."

"*Did she mention a name?*" Max felt perfectly capable of committing murder.

"No name." Jake touched his arm. "I think maybe you and I should—"

"Back off," Max warned Jake, stepping away.

"Come on, Max. I didn't think you'd—"

"Care?" Max barked, turning to glare at Jake.

"Go off the deep end."

"I'm not off the deep end. I'm going to kill the son of a bitch with my bare hands, but I'm not off the deep end."

"I couldn't care less about what you do to some nameless guy. But I'm a little worried about Cara."

"Don't worry about Cara," said Max. He wasn't angry with

Cara. Okay, so maybe he was angry with her. But he wasn't furious with her. He wanted an explanation. And then he wanted to kill someone. And then he wanted to make her forget every other man on the planet.

"I *am* worried," said Jake.

"I'm not going to hurt Cara."

Jake rolled his eyes. "Of *course* you're not going to hurt her. I don't want you upsetting her. I don't want you yelling at her. Gillian told me this in confidence."

Max let out a cold laugh. "Well, you blew that, buddy. Because there's no way in hell I'm going to pretend I don't know."

"Yeah." Jake sighed. "And there was no way in hell I was going to keep it from you." Then Jake gave his head a sad shake. "I really hate to blow my chances with her. I haven't found one single thing I don't like about her." His gaze moved to Gillian and her ring of admirers. "Not one single thing."

Max spat out a pithy swearword. He hated compromising his best friend, but he had no choice here. "I gotta ask her."

"I know you do." Jake looked resigned. "Just don't make it any worse than it has to be, okay?"

"I'll try," Max promised. His feet were already in motion, carrying him across the vast concrete floor toward Cara. He honestly didn't know what he was going to do.

His brain was swirling, his emotions raw, by the time he got to Cara and the vice president.

"I'm sorry," he told the man, voice carefully controlled. "I'm afraid we're running late."

Without giving Cara a moment to react, Max linked her arm in his and all but dragged her away.

"What?" she sputtered, struggling to get her feet sorted out beneath her. She glanced behind them, then she looked up at Max. "Slow *down*."

"Sorry." He measured his pace but kept them on course for the exit.

"Where are we going? What are you doing? What about everyone else?"

"We have to talk."

"About what?"

"Not here."

"Max," she demanded.

"Gillian can ride back with Jake."

There were three NCN production vehicles still sitting in the parking lot outside. Max was taking one for him and Cara. He didn't much care how the others worked it out.

"They had a date last night," he said to Cara. "Did you know they had a date last night?"

"I know they went to a club after dinner." There was confusion in Cara's tone. "Did something happen? Is something wrong? Gillian said she had a good time."

"Nothing happened." But something was terribly, horribly wrong.

Outside in the hot parking lot, Max swung open the passenger door to one of the SUVs.

Cara shook off his hand, turning to face him. "Why are you doing this? What's wrong?"

"Get in."

"I'm not getting in."

"Get in, Cara. We need to talk."

She glared at him a moment longer, but then something in her expression faltered. She paled a shade, then she gave a shaky nod and got into the vehicle without another argument.

It seemed like she'd figured it out, knew that he knew. He sure hoped she was ready to explain herself. Not that any explanation would be satisfactory. They might not have come out and said it, but given all that had happened between them, it was absolutely unconscionable that she should be with another guy.

A fresh wave of anger rolled over Max as he stomped around the front of the SUV, nearly ripping off the driver's door.

Another guy.

Another guy?

What the hell was the *matter* with her?

He stabbed the key into the ignition and tore out of the parking lot, heading down the deserted, industrial road toward the mountain drive.

"Max," Cara began in a small, shaky voice.

"Don't," he warned her. "I can't talk about this and keep us on the road at the same time."

She fell quiet, her fingertips going to her temples.

Max took the curves as fast as he dared. It wasn't until they'd climbed several thousand feet, leaving the city behind, that he pulled off onto a narrow dirt road. He took them far enough that they wouldn't be disturbed, pulled onto a narrow track and stomped on the brakes, rocking the vehicle to a halt.

He shoved it in Park, killed the engine and set the brake. Silence closed in around them, and he could hear the thump of his own heart.

"Max," she tried again.

He turned in his seat and held up a finger to silence her. "Who is he?" he rasped.

She blinked in apparent confusion.

"Who is he?" Each syllable cut through his throat like broken glass.

Cara was shrinking back against the passenger door. "Who is who?" Her voice had turned to a dry rasp.

"I want to kill him, Cara." Max smacked his palm on the steering wheel. "Heaven help me, I want to wrap my hands around his neck and squeeze."

She swallowed convulsively. "Who?"

"The guy. Whoever he is. Whatever guy you've been with—" Max couldn't bring himself to say any more. He turned to face the windshield, gripping hard on the steering wheel.

Long moments went by in silence.

The wind whistled outside, the odd bird sounding in the distance.

He realized he couldn't do this. He was too angry right now. Whatever Cara had done, whatever her motivation, he needed to calm himself down before they talked about it. This wasn't fair to her.

"I'm sorry," he managed, reaching for the key.

"Max, I don't know what you're talking about."

"Gillian," he admitted. Then he turned to look at her again. He didn't want to make things worse for Jake, but the dishonesty had to stop somewhere. "Gillian told Jake you'd been with another guy. It made me angry. Too angry for us to have this conversation."

"Gillian?" Cara's voice was barely a squeak.

"She told him in confidence. He broke that confidence. He thought I should know." Max looked her square in the eyes. "And he was right. I should know. I don't know why you wouldn't tell me." He felt his anger rising all over again. "Hell, I don't know why you would have done it."

Cara blinked rapidly, her eyes taking on a bright sheen. "Max, I—"

"You don't have to explain." He hadn't meant to make her cry. He fought for calm again. He was heartsick but calmer now. And he knew he had to answer for his outburst.

"Gillian shouldn't have said that." A single tear escaped from Cara's bright blue eyes, streaking down in the sunshine that illuminated her face.

Despite everything, the tear ripped at his heart. He couldn't breathe. He could barely speak. "You don't have to tell me anything."

She drew a shaky breath. "There was no other guy."

"Don't lie. Please, just stop talking. I couldn't stand it if you lied to me."

She swiped the back of her hand across her damp cheek. "There was no other guy, Max."

He didn't know what to say to that. He wanted to believe her. He so very desperately wanted to believe her. And she looked sincere. She looked sincere and fragile and more beautiful than ever.

"There hasn't been any other guy since I've been with you. Since before I was with you. Since about a year before I was with you."

Hope flickered inside Max.

She reached out and touched his arm. "Gillian was wrong. She must have misunderstood something… Maybe something I said."

Anger and despair shuddered their way in waves out of Max's body. "Are you serious?"

"Nobody but you, Max." She gave a watery smile. "Nobody but you."

Max couldn't resist. He couldn't stop himself. He reached for her, pulling her across the seat, setting her in his lap, pushing back her hair, stroking her soft cheeks with his thumbs as he bent to kiss her mouth.

Her sweet taste invaded him as relief poured through him. He parted her lips, delving deep, tasting and possessing her essence. He inhaled her scent, felt the softness of her skin on his fingertips and the slight weight of her bottom against his lap.

He was instantly aroused and kissed her again, deeper this time. She kissed him back, a purring sound forming in her throat as her arms encircled his neck. The coolness of her fingers soothed the heat of his skin. The last vestige of his temper vanished, replaced by a driving need to make love to her.

His hands moved to her rib cage, sliding upward, thumbs beneath her round breasts. He plucked at her buttons, freeing her blouse, cupping his palm over the smooth satin of her bra.

She squirmed in his lap.

"Cara," he groaned, wishing she'd protest or smack him away, something, anything to slow this down.

A primal need had hijacked his brain. She was his, his, *his*. There was no way he was going to stop on his own.

But she wasn't slowing this down. Her hands were on his

shirt, releasing his buttons. Between kisses, she gasped for breath. Then she tipped her head back, her teeth biting down on her lip.

He kissed her exposed neck, drawing the succulent skin into the heat of his mouth. Her breasts were soft under his hand, the nipples beading against his palm. His body was on autopilot, free hand reaching beneath her skirt, tugging at her panties, stripping them off.

He touched her, and she groaned, thighs twitching, parting. She moved to straddle him, and her skirt bunched up around her hips.

He drew back an inch, staring into her eyes. They breathed deeply in unison, neither of them saying a word.

He reached for his slacks, unfastening, loosening, until there was no barrier between them.

"Only you," she whispered, the sheen back in her eyes.

"Oh, Cara." He pressed inside her, all rational thought flying from his brain.

Her hot body closed around him, and his hips flexed. He spread his fingers into her hair, bracing her for his kiss, opening wide, delving deep. Her fingernails dug into his shoulder. He wrapped an arm around her waist, pulling her to him, crushing her breasts against his bare chest.

He measured his rhythm, desperate to make it last. He ran his hand across her stomach, along her thighs, to the tender spot behind her knee.

Then he retraced the route, savoring her smooth, soft heat. She gasped at his touch, then moaned softly, pressing herself against his caress.

"You're beautiful," he whispered, increasing his pace. "So incredibly off-the-charts beautiful."

A haze moved through his brain, the world disappearing. Nothing mattered but Cara. Nothing ever would.

"Max," she cried, her breathing turning to quick pants.

"Yes," he groaned, speeding up, struggling to drag oxygen into his own lungs.

Her body stiffened then contracted around him.

"Oh, yes," he gasped, letting himself launch into endless waves of blissful oblivion.

Sounds came back first, the birds and the rustle of the leaves outside. Then came the sweet scent of Cara. Max opened his eyes and blinked against the bright sunshine, waiting for her gorgeous face to come back into focus. Inside the car, the air was stifling and she was slick against his skin.

"Can you breathe?" he asked her.

"Barely."

He managed to flick the ignition key to the accessory setting and press the buttons for the front windows. A welcome breeze flowed over them.

"Thanks." She smiled, pushing back her damp bangs.

He couldn't help but grin, kissing her playfully on the tip of the nose. "You are more than welcome." He paused, sobering. "Anytime."

Her smile also disappeared. "That's not what I meant."

"I know," he acknowledged.

They both went silent, but neither of them moved.

"I didn't plan this," Max told her. It wasn't an apology. He wasn't sorry. But he didn't want her to think he'd driven her into the woods to make love.

"I don't know what to do," she responded in a small voice.

He wasn't sure what she meant. "Right now?"

Her tone was searching. "Always before, I thought I knew. I might not have liked it, but I knew what it was I was supposed to do."

Her gaze studied his. "But we can't date. We sure can't have an affair." She gave a helpless little laugh. "And every time we try to stay away from each other…"

"Fate intervenes?" he offered.

"I don't think we can call this fate."

"I think we can call it anger," he admitted. Then he touched his forehead to hers. "I was so angry, Cara. We might not be officially dating but, apparently, you can't sleep with any other man without me losing it."

"I'm not."

"I know."

"I'm sorry," she whispered.

"You didn't do anything."

Unexpectedly, her arms wound around his neck.

He wrapped his own around her waist and held her close.

"I don't know what to do," she told him again, a catch to her voice.

He stroked his palms up and down her bare back. "You don't have to decide right now. We shouldn't decide right now. We can't."

"We have to do something."

"I'll finish the show, and you'll do your job." He eased back to look at her. "You are amazing."

"I'm a mess." She gave a nervous laugh, wiping her fingertips under her eyes, ineffectually rubbing at her smeared makeup.

Her hair was mussed, her clothes askew. Her cheeks were bright red, and she was covered in a dewy glow in the soft sunshine. He wanted her again already.

But he forced himself to close her blouse, fastening the buttons before he could change his mind.

"We're professionals," he told her. "We'll finish our work here, and we'll go back to D.C. And we won't decide anything, one way or the other, until we have time to think."

He sounded far more confident than he felt. Because he couldn't see any way forward, but he also couldn't see himself giving her up.

Gillian all but hauled Cara over the threshold into her hotel suite. "What happened? Where did you go? Why didn't you answer your phone?"

"Here's one for you," Cara returned as Gillian shut the door behind them. "*What* did you tell Jake?"

Gillian looked confused. "About what?"

"About me. My sex life. Other men in my sex life."

"Oh, that."

"Oh, *that?*" Cara marched into the center of the enormous room and spun around to face her sister.

Gillian seemed confused. "You said you wanted me to do it."

"When? When did I say anything remotely like that?"

"Last night. Right here in the room. We were talking about how you had to start telling people you were pregnant, if only to keep yourself out of danger."

"I said I wouldn't tell Max I was pregnant." Cara remembered it well.

"And I said, 'Max needs to think it's not his baby.' You responded, and I quote, 'Yeah, I know he does.'"

"And you took that to mean you should lie to him?"

"I took that to mean you finally understood what we had to do. And Jake gave me the perfect opening. You'd have been proud, Cara. I slipped it in there like nothing."

"I thought Max knew I was pregnant," Cara told her sister. "When he hauled me away to talk like that, I thought he'd figured it all out. I was about to confess everything."

"But you didn't?"

"I didn't."

Gillian motioned for Cara to follow her to two big armchairs recessed into a bay window overlooking the sunny city. "What did he say? What happened?"

"He was furious." Cara found herself shuddering at the memory.

Gillian sat down and Cara followed suit, sinking into the deep, plush cushions. "I realized he didn't know I was pregnant. But he took *great* exception to the idea of me sleeping with another man."

"Really?" Gillian mused.

"Don't act so surprised."

"Well, it's hardly the 1950s."

"Fidelity doesn't go out of style," said Cara.

"You said the two of you hadn't agreed to be exclusive."

"I'm not promiscuous, either."

Gillian straightened. "I didn't mean to insult you."

Some of the fight went out of Cara. "I know you were try-ing to help. But, man alive, I've never seen anything like it."

"He didn't hurt you?"

"No. No. Nothing like that. But he threatened to kill the guy." Cara let her mind slip back to the conversation. "But then he calmed himself down. I don't think he's used to los-ing his temper. And then…"

Gillian waited.

Cara could feel her cheeks going warm.

"And then?" Gillian prompted, curiosity rising in her blue eyes.

"After I swore there'd been no other guys—"

"You what? Wait. You wasted my perfectly fantastic setup? Why would you tell him there'd been no other guys?"

"I couldn't lie to him, Gilly. For some reason, the one thing in this world I can't do is lie to Max."

"That's ridiculous. He's just a man. You know this puts you right back where you started."

"I'd be thrilled to be back where I started."

Gillian went on alert. "What aren't you telling me?"

Cara tugged a wrinkle out of her skirt. "God, I miss wine." She'd give anything right now for a glass of Merlot, or two or three.

"For the taste or the alcohol?" asked Gillian.

"Do you think they make a baby-safe margarita?"

"Sure. Unfortunately, you have to leave out the tequila." Gillian leaned forward and took Cara's hand. "You slept with him again, didn't you?"

"If by slept, you mean had frantic sex with him in the front seat of his car, yes."

"Makeup sex?"

"Turns out, it really is the very best kind."

Gillian have her a squeeze. "Oh, Cara."

"I know. I'm addicted. I have to do something. I have to take drastic action. Can your jet make it to Australia?" It was the farthest place Cara could think of where they spoke English and she might reasonably get a job in the U.S. embassy.

"With a stopover in Hawaii, sure. You want to go now?"

Cara let herself fantasize for a moment about walking out of this hotel room and getting far, far away. Unfortunately, Max popped up in the middle of the fantasy.

"Can we talk about something else?" she asked Gillian.

A second went by. "Sure."

"My misery needs some company. Please tell me you make mistakes. Have you done anything stupid lately?"

"I did something tacky today."

"Good." Cara settled into the armchair. "Tell me all about it."

"I flirted with the pilots at Manning Aviation."

Cara couldn't help feeling a little disappointed. "How is that tacky? You mean because there were six of them?"

Gillian laughed. "Are you hungry?"

"I'm always hungry."

"Let's get room service." Gillian reached for the cordless phone on the table beside her chair. "What do you want?"

"A milk shake."

"Seriously? Again? Is the pregnancy and ice cream thing true?"

"I don't want pickles." Cara couldn't help but cringe as she imagined the tart taste. "But I'd take a sundae instead of a milk shake. Hot fudge, whipped cream, a cherry on top."

"You're out of control."

"I am."

"What do you really want?"

Cara really wanted a sundae. "Get me a wrap of some kind. And I'll take a salad with it. But I do want the milk shake."

"Is it okay with you if I order wine?"

"No, it's not okay for you to order wine, Auntie Gillian. If I'm staying dry, so are you. Get a milk shake."

Gillian pressed a button on the phone. "If I can't fit into my jeans, it'll be all your fault."

"Do an extra hour at the gym."

Gillian ordered two of everything and then put down the phone.

"Tell me about the tacky flirting," said Cara. She needed something to take her mind off Max, and off the baby, and off her daunting future.

Gillian kicked off her shoes, lifting her feet onto the chair, propping one elbow on her upraised knee. "I was trying to make Jake jealous."

Cara was confused. "I thought he was already interested in you."

"I think he is. A little, anyway. We danced pretty late last night. And it was fun. And he walked me back to the hotel. And then he said good-night at the elevator."

"Did you want him to come up?"

Gillian gave a sheepish shrug. "I wanted him to *want* to come up."

"But you didn't invite him."

"No."

"So he didn't turn you down."

"Please. He's male."

Cara coughed out a laugh. It felt good. "Do you even know what you want?"

"I don't," Gillian admitted. "Okay, I do. He blows hot and cold. One minute, he's all friendly and attentive, and the next minute I might as well be a lawn ornament."

"I think becoming a billionaire has messed with your head," Cara observed.

"I'm not a billionaire."

"You're used to being the center of attention. I bet when you walk into a room, every man snaps to."

"Only because I sign their paychecks."

"But Jake doesn't do it, and it makes you crazy."

Gillian groaned, raking her hands through her hair. "Have I turned into a spoiled princess?"

"Did the pilots flirt back?" asked Cara, struggling not to smile at her sister discomfort.

"Yes. And they weren't there for the interview, so they didn't know who I was. So money or not, I know I've still got it."

"And Jake knows you've got it."

"He does," Gillian agreed.

"Was he jealous?"

"I hope so."

"Are you seeing him again tonight?"

"I don't know. What are you doing?"

"The president is hosting a dinner and welcome reception for the summit heads of state. It's private, about two hundred people. Luckily, no press." Cara glanced at her watch. "I have to get dressed in an hour."

"When are you going back?"

"To D.C.?"

Gillian nodded.

"Tomorrow night, after the closing statements. I'm hitching a ride on Air Force One. I'll be busy every minute between now and then." It was just as well. The less time Cara had to think, the better.

Ten

Max had been back in D.C. for three days.

Though Ariella's brief interview had momentarily taken attention off the president, it had also renewed interest in Eleanor Albert. Max's boss, Nadine, was more determined than ever to find the elusive woman. At the same time, Liam Fisher had come up with solid evidence that somebody from ANS had hacked into a computer in the president's campaign headquarters.

"We don't have a name yet," said Liam, rolling out a chair to take a seat next to Jake at the oval oak table in the NCN boardroom.

"We'll get there," said Max. "At least we know we're on the right track."

There was no evidence yet to implicate owner Graham Boyle, nor was there anything pointing to Marnie Salloway, but Max was still suspicious of his old boss. She'd been vague and smug the last time they spoke, and he was sure she was hiding something. Not that his suspicions got him any closer to the truth.

Nadine breezed into the room, an assistant in tow. "You went way too easy on Caroline Cranshaw in L.A.," she accused Max without preamble.

"She's a pro," Max returned while Nadine sat down. "She wasn't going to give us anything."

Jake slid a glance Max's way, silently indicating that he agreed with Nadine.

"The real story is ANS," said Max, looking to Liam for support. "We know they broke the law."

"We know somebody they once employed broke the law," Nadine retorted. "But we also know they targeted the president in their efforts to find information. That means somebody at the White House knows more than they're letting on."

"No," Max disagreed. "It means ANS *thinks* somebody at the White House knows more than they're letting on."

"And who knows the most about the scandal?" Nadine challenged, drumming her polished fingers on the table top.

Max didn't respond to the rhetorical question.

"ANS knows most about the scandal," Nadine answered her own question. "And they're targeting the White House for information. Eleanor Albert is the story. Find her."

Liam sat forward in his chair, folding his hands on the table, looking both dignified and wise. Even Nadine stopped to listen.

"If this hacking can be traced to ANS," he stated, "if it goes up to the reporters or up to Marnie Salloway or all the way up to Graham Boyle, then NCN has its own scoop."

"*If* they did it," Nadine retorted. "And *if* we can prove it. And *if* we can prove it before anyone else."

"They did it," said Liam with conviction. "And the campaign office is just the tip of the iceberg."

"I'd put money on Marnie having her fingers in this particular pie," Max added.

"Comforting," Nadine drawled sarcastically. "But the Eleanor story is a sure thing. If we find her, we've got a ready-made scoop." She looked at Liam. "She went somewhere after Fields. Even if she died, she did it somewhere."

"On it," Liam agreed, accepting the decision.

Then Nadine turned her attention to Max. "We just did Lynn Larson a big favor."

"I thought it was Lynn Larson who did us a favor." The press secretary could have called any network and made a deal for Ariella's statement.

"You're going down to the White House to collect."

Max immediately thought of Cara at the White House. He suspected she'd been avoiding him since their return from L.A. He knew the entire White House was scrambling to stop the slide in the president's popularity, and the press office was right in the thick of things. Still, he'd left half a dozen messages and she wasn't calling him back.

He missed her more than he could have imagined. The upside of approaching Lynn was that he had a decent chance of seeing Cara. His chest tightened in anticipation.

"Fine," he agreed. "What do you want me to ask her?"

Nadine came to her feet. "You're the investigative journalist. You figure it out."

Her assistant immediately hopped up, following Nadine out the door.

The three men waited a full minute.

"How far can we go investigating ANS on our own?" asked Jake.

Max responded, "Before it turns into flat-out insubordination?"

Liam grinned. "We're fairly safe if we do it after business hours."

"I'm on board," Max agreed.

He knew the best way to help his situation with Cara was to deal with the scandal that was taking all of her time. If they did prove something against ANS, then the public's attention would shift from the president. Cara's time would free up in a heartbeat. As he worked the coming long hours, Max would cling to that.

Cara paused in Lynn's office to stare at the biggest of the television screens on the office wall.

"In a fascinating twist that's seen the president's popularity drop even further," the pretty, blond female announcer cooed from the center of a small crowd at the front gate of the White House, "Madeline Schulenburg, a forty-six-year-old woman who grew up in Doublecreek, Montana, some two hours away from the president's hometown of Fields, is claiming her twenty-eight-year-old son was fathered by Ted Morrow."

Cara set the draft report from the Los Angeles trip on Lynn's desk. "I guess it was only a matter of time."

"Until the crazies came out?" Lynn swiveled in her high-backed desk chair to face Cara.

"There's no chance this is true, right?"

"I don't know what's true anymore," Lynn admitted, twisting her ring.

"It can't be." Though Cara supposed it was possible. Maybe there were two illegitimate children. Then again, why not three or four?

"Have you spoken to the president?" she asked her boss.

"That's what I get to do right now," Lynn rose to her feet, gathering a couple of files from her desktop. "Mr. President," she mumbled in a mocking tone. "On the Madeline Schulenburg situation. Can we talk about your sex life? Again?"

"So the White House is taking this seriously" came a deep voice from Lynn's open doorway.

Lynn's head whipped up, and Cara whirled to come face-to-face with Max.

"Who let you in here?" Lynn demanded.

Cara couldn't find her voice. She'd been working sixteen-hour days since Los Angeles, and it was still a fight to keep

Max from her mind. She missed him. And she was desperately confused and worried about the future.

"I have an appointment," said Max.

"Sandy was supposed to cancel," said Lynn.

"Is it true?" asked Max. "Is there another illegitimate child? Is the White House expecting more of them to surface?"

"Go away," said Lynn.

"Shall I put you down for a no comment?" asked Max.

Lynn squared her shoulders, glaring hard at Max. "Cara, would you please show the nice reporter out of the building?"

The request shook Cara back to life. "Yes." She moved toward Max. "Of course. Come with me, please." She gestured to the hallway.

"What's going on?" he muttered in her ear.

"Go," she ordered in a low growl.

She and Max headed straight down the hallway, while Lynn took a right toward the Oval Office.

Before she could stop him, Max ducked into her own office.

"Max," she called, quickly following to protect the information that sat exposed on her desk.

She crossed the small room, flipping over reports and closing file folders.

"Talk to me, Cara."

She turned. "I have nothing to say."

"If there are more children…"

"There are not," she told him with conviction.

"You're lying." He cocked his head, watching her intently.

She felt her pulse jump, and a funny buzz formed in the pit of the stomach that had nothing to do with the president.

Max took a step forward.

The buzz turned to genuine fear, and she sharply held up a hand. "Don't."

"So," he mused, coming to a stop far too close to her for comfort. "Either you're lying because the president has more secret children or because you don't know one way or the other."

"You have to leave, Max." She meant that on many different levels.

They couldn't discuss the president, and she didn't dare spend time in Max's company. Even now, even in the middle of the West Wing, in the midst of a crisis, she wanted to throw herself into his arms.

He lowered his voice. "I need to see you."

She shook her head. "That can't happen."

"Not here," he clarified. "Later. Tonight. At your place."

"No."

"We have to talk."

"I'm working tonight. And tomorrow night." And every night into the foreseeable future.

"You have to sleep sometime."

"Not with—" She snapped her jaw shut.

A twinkle came into his green eyes. "With me would definitely be my preference."

She tried to back away, but she was blocked by her desk. "This isn't a joke."

"I'm not joking. I miss you, Cara." He eased even closer.

She steeled herself, trying desperately to quash her feelings. She couldn't want Max. She couldn't touch him or talk to him, or even see him.

"You promised, Max," she told him in a pleading voice, looking straight into his eyes.

"I just want to talk."

"You're lying."

"You're right."

Voices sounded outside in the hall, and Cara quickly slipped sideways, putting some distance between them.

Max's glance dropped to her desktop. His blatant curiosity gave her a last burst of emotional strength.

"You're here investigating the story," she stated.

"I am," he admitted.

"Get out of my office, Max. Or I'll call security."

This time, he did take a step back. "Okay. I'll call you later."

"I won't answer."

"I'll try anyway."

And then he was gone.

Cara gripped the lip of the desk to steady herself. She took a few bracing breaths. It was obvious she couldn't be trusted around Max. It was just as obvious that he wasn't going to stay away from her.

She made her way around the desk, sitting down to face her computer terminal. There she brought up the human resources page. She entered a search, checking to see what public relations jobs were currently available in foreign embassies.

To her surprise, there was an opening in Australia.

The optimism that had stayed with Max since he'd made love to Cara in Los Angeles evaporated as he walked off the White House grounds. She was never going to listen to reason. She was never going to give the two of them a chance. She'd decided their relationship was impossible, and she wasn't going to explore any evidence to the contrary.

His only choices were to move on with his own life or to settle in for a long wait and spend the next four years campaigning against the president so that Cara would be free after the next election. Problem was, he didn't think he could wait four years, never mind eight.

He made his way to his Mustang, hit the remote to unlock the door, climbed into the driver's seat and extracted his phone from his pocket. He quashed the feelings for Cara that were messing with his reporter's instincts and entered the Georgetown address he'd seen scrawled across the yellow pad of paper on her desktop. She was meeting with someone in less than an hour.

He started his car, cranking up the heat against the gray,

blowing January day. He scrolled through the search results, discovering the address was in a medical building. More specifically, it was an obstetrics practice. Another quick search told Max the practice had been there for at least thirty years.

It struck him as odd that an obstetrician in D.C. would be involved in babies from Montana. But maybe the doctor had moved. Or maybe one of the mothers had ended up in D.C. They knew for certain in Eleanor's case that she'd hightailed it out of Fields while she was newly pregnant.

He pressed the speed dial button for Jake.

"Yeah?" came Jake's short greeting.

"I've got something," said Max.

"Eleanor?"

"No. Maybe something on her. But don't discount that the rumors of other children might be true. Lynn Larson's pretty rattled by the latest story."

"What do you need?" asked Jake.

"I'm heading for Georgetown. An obstetrics practice. I don't want to spook anyone by showing up with a camera, but can you be on standby in the neighborhood in case there's a doctor there who'll talk?"

"Sure. I'm with Liam, but we're just finishing up. Text me the address."

"Coming at you," Max promised.

He ended the call, sent Jake the address, then exited the parking lot. It took a while to negotiate the slushy, crowded streets, but he managed to find the medical building. He then searched out a parking spot and found one several blocks away.

Partway back to the front entrance of the six-story, brownstone, he spotted Cara exiting a taxi. He glanced at his watch. She was a good fifteen minutes early for her meeting. Too bad. He'd hoped to beat her inside and figure out which doctor or nurse or whoever she'd found who might know something.

Instead, he hung back. He gave her enough time to make it

through the halls and hopefully clear the waiting room. Then he followed.

The suite was on the sixth floor. The directory sign at the top of the elevator took him to the far end of the hallway to a set of double, frosted glass doors. He opened them slowly and glanced around a brightly lit, cheerfully decorated waiting room.

Three very pregnant women sat in the padded chairs, leafing through parenting magazines. Two other women held babies in their laps; one of them kept a sharp eye on a toddler playing with toys in a corner.

Max slipped inside, drawing the interest of the nurse behind the counter. The sign above her listed four doctors.

Trying to look like he belonged, Max moved toward the nurse's smiling face.

"How can I help you?" She peered at him above her reading glasses. Happily, there was no recognition in her eyes. She obviously wasn't an *After Dark* viewer.

Max hesitated, not knowing what to ask. There was absolutely no way to know which doctor to approach. It could be another staff member. It seemed unlikely that it was the nurse herself, or Cara would be out here talking.

Then inspiration struck him. "I'm here with Caroline Cranshaw." He pretended to search his pockets. "It's been a really busy day, and I'm afraid I've lost the name—"

"Oh, you're the *father*." The woman grinned as if she'd seen it all before.

Max's brain skipped a beat.

"She's talking with Dr. Murdoch in his office right now. You can feel free to join them." The nurse pointed. "Straight down the blue hallway. Dr. Murdoch's name is on the office door."

Max blinked in shock. Would Cara have actually lied about being pregnant to get in to see an obstetrician?

What was she, under deep cover? Good grief, she was a public relations specialist, not a private investigator.

"Right that way," the nurse reiterated. "The blue hallway."

"Thanks," Max told her, turning to go.

Cara was going to be ticked off, but he had to follow this lead. She'd made it more than clear that a relationship between them wasn't happening, and he had his professional integrity to think about. He couldn't let his feelings for her cloud his judgment any longer.

Cara had far too much power over his actions, and that was about to stop.

He made his way down the hall.

He gave a cursory knock on the doctor's office door, then opened it up.

The fiftysomething doctor looked up in surprise, and Cara turned her head at the sound.

She froze for a long second. Then her face blanched white, and her blue eyes grew to nearly twice their usual size.

"Hello, darling," he drawled, closing the door behind her. If she could lie, then so could he. If he pretended to be the father, she could hardly call him on it without exposing her own dishonesty.

The doctor looked at Cara for a second, then refocused his attention on Max.

Max strode forward as if he had every right to be there. He held out his hand to the doctor. "Max Gray. I'm sorry I'm late."

For good measure, he planted a quick kiss on the top of Cara's head before taking the chair beside her.

"Max," she rasped, swallowing. "How did you know?"

He smiled broadly and patted her hand. "You told me about the appointment. I know I forget things sometimes, but this is important, darling."

She blinked in what was obviously complete and utter confusion.

"Max Gray? From *After Dark?*" the doctor asked.

"Yes," Max responded easily.

"Nice to meet you." The doctor got back down to business.

"I was just saying to Caroline that I don't anticipate any complications. She's at a great age for a first child. There are no underlying health concerns. I've prescribed a prenatal vitamin, and we'll do the usual blood work. But otherwise, there's nothing special she needs to worry about for the next couple of months."

The doctor fell silent.

Max glanced back at Cara, wondering how long she was going to keep this up. How did she expect to segue from a fake pregnancy into questions about the president's illegitimate children?

She was still staring at him, completely still and obviously dumbfounded.

"Cara?" He waved a hand in front of her face.

She didn't react.

"Caroline?" The doctor rose to come around the desk. He took her hand. "Is something wrong?"

"How did you know?" she whispered to Max.

Something in her eyes turned Max's stomach to stone.

Wait.

No.

No, it couldn't be.

But he'd been an investigative reporter too long to ignore what his gut instinct was telling him.

He looked to the doctor, framing a slow, carefully worded question. "You did a pregnancy test here in the office?"

"Of course," the man responded. "We always confirm the home pregnancy test results. Our best estimate is seven weeks."

Cara was pregnant.

And she hadn't slept with anyone else. She had made that perfectly clear.

She was pregnant with Max's child.

The floor beneath him shifted, and he nearly fell out of his chair. He managed to stand on shaky legs, motioning vaguely to the door.

"I'm going to…" he managed. "I'll meet you…" He flicked a glance at Cara's stricken expression and swiftly left the office.

He walked through the waiting room, his mind a crush of conflicting emotions. He'd invaded Cara's privacy in an absolutely unforgivable way. But she'd lied to him. She'd kept him completely in the dark. And he was going to be a father.

As he pressed the elevator button, the world around him grew fuzzy and indistinct. He was in no way, shape or form in a position to become a father. He'd made that more than abundantly clear.

Cara opened the door of her apartment to greet her sister, trying valiantly to put on a brave face. "You can't just jump in your jet every time my life has a hiccup."

"This is more than a hiccup." Gillian pulled Cara into a tight hug. "This is a catastrophe."

Cara pointedly looked up the spiral staircase. "Ariella and Scarlet are here."

"Do they know?"

Cara started to shake her head.

"Do we know what?" came Ariella's voice from above.

The two women appeared at the top of the stairs, peering down. Scarlet was Cara's close friend, a D.C. party planner she had known for years.

Neither Cara nor Gillian answered the question.

"What don't we know?" asked Ariella.

"You might as well tell them." Gillian shut the door and shrugged out of her black coat. "They're your friends, and they love you."

"Whatever it is, you'd better tell us," Ariella said as she descended the stairs.

"I've applied for an embassy job in Australia," said Cara with a warning look at Gillian not to share more.

"You're doing what?" Scarlet gasped from up-top.

"What on earth?" Ariella asked. "Why would you do that?"

Gillian folded her arms across her chest, arching a brow in Cara's direction.

"Fine," Cara capitulated, deciding it was time to face up to the reality of her future.

"Because she's pregnant," Gillian put in.

"What?" Ariella shrieked.

"Well, that was blunt," Cara told her sister.

"There's no point in beating around the bush," Gillian returned. "It'll be obvious in a few weeks. And even if you leave the country, they're going to notice next Christmas when you show up with a baby."

"Who says I'm coming to D.C. for Christmas?"

"Back up, back up," Ariella insisted.

"Are we going to stand here and talk about this in the entry hall?" asked Gillian.

"We're not." Scarlet motioned to them. "Get up here and tell us what's going on."

Ariella pivoted to head back up the stairs. Cara followed, and Gillian brought up the rear.

"Has he called yet?" asked Gillian.

"Who?" Ariella and Scarlet asked in unison.

Cara turned on her sister. "Are you going to lay my entire life bare here?"

"We want to help you," said Ariella.

"And we sure don't want you to leave D.C.," Scarlet added.

There was a note of sincerity in each of their voices that tugged at Cara's heart. She knew she could trust her friends. Maybe their support was exactly what she needed right now.

"I am pregnant," Cara admitted as the women made their way to the living room and settled onto the sofas and into armchairs.

"How far along?" asked Ariella.

"Seven weeks," Cara answered Ariella.

"What does being pregnant have to do with leaving town?" asked Scarlet.

"She needs to get away from the father," Gillian said.

"Is he nasty?" asked Scarlet.

"Who is he?" asked Ariella.

"Max Gray," Cara admitted, deciding it was time to get everything out on the table. She was going to have to make some significant changes in her life. Keeping any of this a secret was no longer a viable option. "It's Max Gray."

"Seriously?" asked Scarlet, a note of awe in her voice. Cara realized Scarlet saw Max only as a television personality and one of the top ten hottest men in D.C.

"He's not nasty," Ariella put in staunchly. "Max is a great guy."

"The biggest problem is that he doesn't want children," Gillian explained.

"So what?" said Ariella. "He's getting one anyway."

"The biggest problem is the conflict of interest," Cara corrected her sister.

"The baby is a conflict of interest?" asked Scarlet in obvious confusion.

"I can't have a relationship with Max. He's a reporter. I work at the White House."

Ariella sat up straighter on the sofa. "I don't understand. You're not in a relationship with him already?"

"I'm not," Cara affirmed.

"Then how did it happen?" Scarlet seemed to search for an explanation. "Are you his groupie?"

Cara couldn't help but laugh a little hysterically at that suggestion. It might have been easier if it was a one-night stand.

"They dated a while ago," Gillian put in. "Before the election."

Cara sobered. "But it's over."

Scarlet glanced around the circle of friends. "That doesn't matter. He has to step up and take responsibility."

Cara subconsciously moved her hand to her stomach. "I'm

not about to foist an innocent baby onto an unwilling father. I'm not even sure how he found out."

"I am," said Gillian.

Cara turned to her sister in surprise.

"I talked to Jake. Max went to the doctor's office because he thought you were following up on a lead about the president."

Cara's mind went back to Max's odd behavior. "He didn't know?" she ventured.

"Not when he arrived. He was going along with what he thought was your ruse."

"Until he asked about the test." Cara remembered Max's reaction to the doctor's words.

Her heart sank. He'd found out she was pregnant right there in the doctor's office, and he had immediately walked away. It confirmed everything she'd ever feared.

"He feels guilty for invading your privacy," said Gillian.

Cara came to her feet, struggling against an unexpected surge of hurt and anger. "Invading my privacy? *That's* what he feels guilty about? Not because I'm pregnant? Not because he's abandoning his child? Not because he doesn't care one whit about either of us?"

"I don't know how clearly he's thinking right now," said Gillian.

"Max can stuff it." Cara paced across the room, trying to bring her emotions back under control. Forget Max. She was going to deal with this on her own, far away, where she wouldn't be tempted by him or hurt by him ever again. "I'm out of here."

"You can't leave us," cried Scarlet.

"Well, I can't stay here." Cara returned to the armchair and plunked back down, feeling exhausted. "He's never going to change."

"He feels bad about that, too," said Gillian.

"Good for him," Cara snapped.

"If you're not hiding the pregnancy," Ariella offered reasonably, "then get another job in D.C."

"What other job?" asked Cara. "Any job in the White House is going to have the same problem."

"Work for me," said Gillian. "You can do whatever you want if you work for me."

"Very charitable of you, big sister. But you're not in D.C. And I'm not taking your handout."

"Then work for us," said Scarlet.

"Public relations for a party planner?" Cara scoffed.

"Not full-time," Scarlet continued. "And you wouldn't have to be in the office very often. You could work from home. Be a mom." She snapped her fingers. "Open a public relations consulting firm."

"We'd hire you in a heartbeat," said Ariella. "You could set your own hours, do a ton of the work right here in the apartment."

"I don't know." But Cara could see that it would solve one of her problems. Well, two of her problems really. It would get her out of the White House and it would give her more time with her baby.

But Max would still be in D.C. She'd still be hopelessly attracted to him. And it would hurt her to see him and know he didn't want them.

"Are you in love with him?" Scarlet asked softly.

"No," said Cara.

"Yes," said Gillian.

Cara glared at her sister, but Gillian just spread her hands, palms facing the ceiling. "What exactly do you think this is?"

"I am not in love with Max," Cara stated with authority. "I'm simply carrying his baby and fighting some kind of physical obsession over having sex with him."

"Everybody wants to sleep with him," said Scarlet.

Three gazes swung toward her.

"I'm not saying me personally," she hastily put in. "I'm

saying most of the females across the country have the hots for him."

"She's not wrong," said Ariella. Then Ariella turned to Cara. "You can't leave me. Not now. Not with all of this going on. You know more about politics than any of us, and I am absolutely going to need your help and advice."

Her words helped to put Cara's own problems into perspective.

"You're the president's daughter, aren't you?" Scarlet asked Ariella.

"I'm afraid I might be," said Ariella.

Cara's heart went out to her friend. While she might be able to quit the White House, Ariella had been about to be involuntarily swept up in a whirlwind.

Cara realized it was true. Ariella needed her. She also realized her friends were in Washington. Her life was in Washington. Australia might have been a nice fantasy, but it wasn't a good reality.

"I'll stay and help," Cara found herself promising.

Somehow, she'd summon the strength to stay away from Max. Who knew, maybe her feelings would fade and everything would be all right. Maybe Gillian was wrong about Cara being in love. Gillian might be a genius, but there were a few times when she was wrong.

There was a chance this could be one of them.

Eleven

Max sat across from Jake at O'Donovan's, an Irish tavern in Georgetown about a mile from the NCN studios.

"I can't believe you haven't spoken to her yet," Jake said, spinning his heavy beer mug in a circle on the polished wood table.

Max shifted in his red leather armchair. "I don't know what to say to her."

"It's been three days."

"She knows it's been three days." Max took a swig of his half-full mug of Irish stout.

"You think you're a comedian?" Jake demanded.

"I think this is none of your damn business."

"I'm your friend."

"Then you should know when to butt out."

A group of college-aged girls giggled as they made their way past the table toward the high stools at the brass-railed bar. Sconce lights and shelves of exotic whisky and leather-bound books decorated the dark wood walls. A picture of the establishment's founder, Angus O'Donovan, flanked by gold-flecked mirrors, hung in prominence behind the two bartenders.

"A good friend never butts out," Jake said.

"What do you think I should say? Do you want me to offer her money?" Max would do that, of course. Financially, his child would never want for a thing.

"You could start with, 'We're having a baby. Let's talk about what we should do.'"

"And open myself up to virtually anything she might ask?" Max couldn't stand the thought of having to say no to anything, of letting Cara down, of seeing the hurt and disappointment in her eyes. "I'd make a terrible father," he repeated for about the hundredth time.

"Why?" Jake reached for a handful of peanuts. "Seriously, why?"

"I don't like kids," Max opened with the obvious.

Jake seemed to ponder that.

"I have a dangerous job that might kill me at any moment," Max continued. "Cara would spend half her life waiting to become a widow. I had zero in the way of paternal role models. I haven't a clue how to even go about talking to a kid. I'm genetically unsuited to fatherhood. When the going gets tough, the Gray men get gone."

"All true," Jake unexpectedly agreed.

"You see my point?"

"I do."

Max rested his hand on his beer mug. "So this conversation is over."

"You still have to talk to her."

Max's stomach clenched, and his jaw hardened in frustration. "And say *what*?"

"She knows all that other stuff, right?"

Max gave a sharp nod. Then he drained his glass.

"Then offer her money." Jake's tone was flat with condemnation. "If that's all you've got, offer to pay her to raise your kid all by herself."

Something stabbed in Max's chest.

Jake wasn't finished. "But look her in the eye, Max. Be a man about it, and tell her in person exactly what you will and won't do for this baby. She didn't get pregnant all by herself, but it sure sounds like that's the way she'll be coping with it."

Max pushed his beer mug away, his stomach going sour.

He caught a movement in his peripheral vision, and Gillian suddenly appeared at the table. Max nearly gave himself whiplash looking around to see if Cara was with her.

She wasn't.

"Did you talk to him?" Gillian asked Jake.

Jake rose, placing a hand loosely at the small of her back. "I did."

Max pushed back his chair and came to his feet. "That was all for her?" he demanded.

"Yeah," said Jake. "That was all for her. Doesn't make it any less true."

"You took me out to the woodshed to get in good with Gillian?"

"No," Gillian responded for Jake. "He's in good with Gillian, and that's why he took you out to the woodshed." She leaned a little closer to Max. "You going to hurt my baby sister?"

"I already did," Max admitted.

"Undo it," said Gillian.

Max shook his head. He couldn't undo it. It was out of his control.

"She applied for an embassy communications job in Australia," Gillian told him.

Max's heart slammed into the side of his chest. "What? Why?"

"So you wouldn't have to be bothered with your baby. She thought it was a good idea to get far, far away."

Max recoiled. But it was a good thing, right? He wouldn't be nearby to mess anything up. The baby would be well cared for, and he could carry on with his life as normal.

Gillian pointed her index finger at Max's chest. "I can see what you're thinking. Don't you dare try to stop her. Don't you dare mess it up."

"Why would I mess it up?" Stopping Cara from leaving D.C. would be foolish. She was separating them. That was a smart move. He'd always known she was smart.

"You messed it up before," Gillian continued. "She wanted you to think there was another guy. You do realize that was the plan, right? If you thought there was another guy, you could tell yourself it wasn't your baby, and you could walk away without worrying about her."

"You lied on purpose?" Max demanded.

"I was your patsy?" Jake asked in obvious surprise.

"Sorry," Gillian said to Jake.

"Here I felt guilty for betraying your secret."

"I knew you would," said Gillian.

"You knew I'd feel guilty?" asked Jake.

"I knew you'd blab to Max. I was counting on it. It was part of the master plan."

"Really?" asked Jake in obvious admiration.

"Really," Gillian answered.

"You're amazing," Jake responded with a sappy grin.

"When does Cara leave?" asked Max.

Not that he needed to know. Or maybe he did. Was Jake right? Did Max owe it to Cara to at least have a conversation? Even if he had nothing but money to offer, should he do it in person? And would she even listen to him if he tried?

Expecting Gillian, Cara was shocked to open her apartment door to Max. Determined as she was, after talking with Gillian, Ariella and Scarlet, to move forward in her new life, she'd cried into her pillow most of last night. Morning hadn't looked much brighter.

He was the last person she wanted to cope with. But standing in the hallway, he looked as tired and hollow as she felt. And she couldn't quite quash a rush of sympathy.

"We need to talk, Cara." He looked like a man headed for the gallows.

She braced herself, determined to get this over with quickly. "No, we don't have to talk. It's fine, Max. There's nothing left to say and nothing left for you to do."

"You're pregnant," he rasped, looking every bit as frightened as he had in Fields when the avalanche hit.

"Yes, I am," Cara confirmed, proud of her matter-of-fact tone. "And I'm fine with that. I truly am. I've made plans."

"So I heard."

"You did?" That surprised Cara.

"From Gillian."

"Oh."

Dear sister Gillian yet again. She'd obviously called Jake last night, thereby sending every word down the überefficient communications pipeline to Max.

"Can I come in?" he asked.

Cara couldn't hold back a frustrated sigh. "Really, Max, I'd rather you—"

But he stepped inside, causing her to step backward to avoid touching him.

"Well, okay, fine," she capitulated. "Come on in."

He closed the door, pressing his back up against it.

"I'm sorry," he began, his glance flicking to her stomach.

"I'm not," she told him with determination.

Amid all the uncertainty and chaos, Cara had come to understand at least one thing. She wasn't sorry about this baby. She was going to be a good mother.

"I meant I was sorry for barging into the doctor's office. I thought you were talking about the president."

"Gillian told me."

"It was a horrible invasion of your privacy, and I don't know what I was thinking." Then some of the fear and defensiveness left his eyes. "But you should have told me you were pregnant."

"Really?" She honestly wasn't sure about that. "Don't you think you'd be better off not knowing? All it's done is make you feel guilty. Knowing the truth hasn't changed your opinion about being a father. It's not going to change your behavior toward the baby."

"Were you really planning to keep it from me? Forever?"

Cara gave a small shrug. That had seemed like her most reasonable plan.

"By leaving the country?" he asked.

"Yes."

"You'd just up and leave me?" he asked, a funny tone coming into his voice.

"*Leave* you? How could I leave you, Max? We were never together. You and me were a nonstarter from minute one."

She could quit work at the White House, getting rid of the conflict of interest. But Max didn't want to be a father. And since she was definitely going to be a mother, the gulf between them was as wide as ever.

He lifted his hand. For a minute, she expected him to touch her face, the way he'd done a hundred times. Stroke his broad palm gently across her cheek, cup her face, draw her in for a kiss.

She could almost feel his fingertips, his full lips coming down on hers.

But he didn't do it. He dropped his hand instead, and her chest tightened in disappointment.

"What do you want, Max?"

"I have money," he told her.

"Really? Being a television star pays well, does it?"

"I meant you and the baby will never want for anything. You'll never have to worry."

Cara swallowed against her tightening throat. She swore to herself that she wouldn't break down. She needed to get this over with as quickly as possible without losing her dignity.

"Thank you, Max," she offered simply.

He frowned. "I might not be able to be with you, but I'll make sure…"

She waited, but he didn't finish the sentence.

"Thank you," she forced out again.

He raised his hand again. This time, it was to rake his fingers through his hair. "Seriously?" he asked her.

Cara didn't understand.

He pivoted on one foot, taking two paces across the small foyer, his voice growing stronger. "That's your reaction?"

"My reaction to what?"

He turned. "Some stupid jerk stands here in front of you and offers you nothing but money to raise his baby all on your own, and you thank him?"

"Are you mad at me?"

"Yes!"

"Why?"

He had no right to be angry. She was making this as easy as possible on him. If anyone deserved to be mad, it was her.

He moved back in front of her. "Tell me no, Cara. Tell me off. Tell me that's not good enough. Hit me or something." His tone rose. "Tell me what you want from me."

"Nothing," she assured him with conviction. "I don't want a single thing from you, Max. We don't need your money. I don't want your charity. The baby and I are going to be perfectly fine, thank you very much."

"Without me?"

"Yes, without you."

Wasn't that the entire point of the conversation?

"In Australia?" Max drawled sarcastically.

Cara was confused. "Who said we were going to Australia?"

"It just occurred to me this very second that this is exactly what you want."

"Huh?"

"For me to go away quietly, to leave you alone, to stay out of your and the baby's life."

Cara stepped closer. "Max, you are losing your mind."

He glared at her for a long moment. His eyes went from glittering emeralds to a stormy sea to dull jade.

"Don't let me do it," he finally said.

"Have you been drinking?"

"Don't let me walk away."

"I'm not *letting* you do anything."

Max was making his own choices. They had nothing to do with her. She couldn't force him one way or another, even if she'd wanted to.

His tone went dull with disgust. "If I walk away from you, I'm no better than my old man."

All the fight went out of Cara. Her entire body congealed into one big ache, and her tone went dead flat. "That's not a reason to stay."

She wouldn't want him under those circumstances.

They stared at each other in charged silence. Then he reached for her hand. She glanced down, hating the way his touch brought her whole body to life.

"I love you, Cara," he whispered in what sounded like amazement. "Do you suppose that's a reason to stay?"

Her stunned gaze flew back to his.

He coughed out a brief, confused laugh. "How about that? I love you so much I can't even think straight. And I am so sorry I didn't realize it until now."

His words weren't computing in her brain.

"Max, what are you saying?"

"I'm saying that I'm not letting you go. I can't let you go. I could never let you go." His free hand went to her stomach. "And I'm not leaving our baby."

Her mind flew into a whirl.

Before she could clear it, he'd moved closer still.

"You can't leave the country," he told her.

"I'm not leaving the country. Max, what is going on here?" She was trying desperately not to hope. But it sounded like he was talking about a future together.

"I'm having an epiphany," he told her. "And it feels great."

"But you don't want a baby."

"Theoretically, no. And there are a lot of logical reasons for that. But you're not theoretical, and neither is our baby. So I've changed my mind."

"Just like that?" she challenged.

"Yes."

"In the past two minutes?"

"Yes. Try to keep up, Cara. I'm in love with you. Did I mention that? Let me say it again. I love you very, very much."

"But—"

He brushed his thumb across her lips to silence her. "I was an idiot. But I'm over it now. Maybe it was Jake's lecture. Maybe it was seeing you. Maybe the thought of you leaving D.C."

"I'm not leaving D.C.," she repeated.

"Gillian said you were moving to Australia."

"Gillian lies quite a lot." Cara was going to have to talk to her sister about that.

Max smiled. "I'm going to kiss you now."

Cara scrambled to wrap her mind around his words. "Are you saying what I think you're saying?"

"If you think I'm saying that I love you, I'm not leaving you, I want to have a baby with you and I'm about to kiss you, then yes, I'm saying what you think I'm saying."

Cara couldn't stop a smile from forming on her face. The aches and pains evaporated from her body, her heart beginning to hope. "Kiss me, Max."

He dipped his head, voice dropping to a whisper. "When I'm finished, you better be ready to tell me that you love me back."

His lips touched hers, and she felt his unabashed love spread through every corner of her body. One of his arms went around her waist, drawing her close, while the other hand stayed protectively cupped around her stomach.

His mouth opened, lips parting hers, his tongue teasing her senses, while his warmth and strength engulfed her from head to toe.

Her arms wound around his neck, and she clung to him as the kiss went on and on.

He finally drew back.

"I love you," burst from a place deep in her chest.

Max smiled. "Thank goodness." He smoothed back her hair. "That'll make it so much easier for you to marry me."

Cara's jaw dropped open.

"I don't have a ring. But I can get one in the next ten minutes if that's a deal breaker. I don't know how we'll make this work with our jobs, but we will. You're my number one priority." He glanced down. "You and the baby."

"You don't like babies," she couldn't help pointing out.

"I'll like your baby. I'll love our baby. I promise, Cara, I will love our baby every second of every day. And I won't die and leave the two of you alone. War-torn cities and crocodiles are in my past."

"You can't uproot your entire life on a whim, Max." Cara was starting to get nervous. This was too much, too fast. It was too perfect.

"It's not a whim. It's a long-overdue brick to the side of my head. I love you so much, Cara. I'm not my father. I promise I won't make his mistakes. Nothing matters to me but you."

Cara began to believe him.

"I quit my job," she told him softly. "I no longer work for the White House. So we don't have a conflict of interest anymore."

He drew her close once again, hugging her tight. "No conflict?"

"No conflict."

"So, I can stay here?"

"Tonight?" Cara would love nothing better than to spend the night in Max's arms.

"Forever."

Three nights later, Cara and Max were back at the Worthington Hotel ballroom. It was a fundraiser for the local school district and Gillian's last night in Washington. She'd made a sizable donation to the computer technology program, while Max had been invited as a local celebrity.

It would be one of Max's last appearances as the host of *After Dark*. He'd told Nadine that he was happy to stay on with the network in another capacity, but he wouldn't be traveling to dangerous parts of the world to capture the stories that had become *After Dark's* trademark.

Happily, Nadine had asked him to take an advisory role. He was going to continue to work on both the Eleanor Albert and the ANS angles. Nadine also told him she had her eye on two up-and-coming investigative reporters as rising stars for the network. The young men were handsome, energetic and fearless.

Max would also advise on the updated version of *After Dark*. The young men were beside themselves with excitement. Max had confessed to Cara that his biggest worry was keeping them from taking too many chances. Then he told her they reminded him of himself when he was younger.

Lynn had been disappointed to lose Cara's communications skills. But, luckily, she was a closet romantic who believed strongly in family. She was thrilled by the prospect of both a wedding and a new baby.

The school fundraiser speeches were over, the dinner dishes cleared away and the waitstaff was now serving individual, three-layered, triple chocolate mousse. Each of the beautiful desserts were topped with berries, spun sugar and a spiral straw of white and dark chocolate.

Cara's appetite was still healthy, and her mouth watered shamelessly in anticipation of such decadence. So, when her dessert was put down in front of her, she immediately scooped up her fork.

Max was watching her, a smug little smile on his face. She also realized she had Gillian's and Jake's attention, as well as the attention of the other four people at the round table.

Was it that surprising for a woman to want dessert?

She frowned at Max.

He simply grinned in return.

Deciding to ignore them, she sliced her dessert fork into the edge of the creamy concoction.

Then something caught her eye, something shiny and sparkling glinting in the light from the overhead chandeliers.

Cara squinted, tilting her head to find a gorgeous diamond ring had been dropped over the chocolate straw and was resting against a plump strawberry. The band was woven white-and-yellow gold, inset with tiny white diamonds, all topped with a spectacular pink solitaire, the same shade as the earrings Max had given to her for Christmas.

She stilled, then smiled, raising her loving gaze to his. "How did you get the stones to match?"

"I called in a favor. A guy I met at the Argyle Mine. They expressed it up."

The entire table breathed a collective "Aw."

He deftly removed the ring from the dessert.

"I'm still eating that," she informed him through her wide grin.

"Eat as many as you like. But give me your hand first."

She held out her left hand, and he slipped the ring onto her finger, sealing it with a kiss.

The table erupted in applause, and Cara could feel her cheeks heat in self-consciousness.

She held out her hand to admire the subtle color, loving the way it sparkled against her finger.

"Like it?" asked Max.

"I love it." She leaned toward him, and he met her kiss halfway.

"I love you," he whispered in her ear.

"Me, too," she whispered back.

When she straightened in her seat, conversation had resumed around the table. Next to her, Gillian was waiting to see the ring.

"Nice," she said to Max with a nod of approval.

"Thank you." Then he paused. "Not that I'm going to believe a word you say ever again."

"All the lies were for your own good," she offered.

"Australia?" he asked, capturing Cara's hand once more to hold it in his.

"She *did* apply for a new job," Gillian assured him. "At least until Ariella, Scarlet and I talked her out of it."

"So I should thank you?"

Gillian shrugged her slim shoulders, bare beneath the spaghetti straps of her ivory gown. "Considering how each of my lies ended, I'd say you should thank me very much."

Max laughed out loud.

"I'm eating my dessert now," Cara announced, lifting her fork to dig in. The mousse was sweet and creamy on her tongue, and she moaned in appreciation.

"Is it time for us to leave?" asked Max, glancing at his watch.

"You're contractually obligated to stay until nine," Cara reminded him. Not that she had any objection to returning to her apartment. The pregnancy was still making her tired early, and sleeping in Max's arms was more of an indulgence than the triple chocolate mousse.

"Since this is my last celebrity gig, I'm perfectly willing to break the contractual terms."

"When's your final show?" Gillian asked.

"Next Friday. After that, I go back to ordinary, anonymous life. Not that life will ever be ordinary with Cara."

"Nice save," Cara told him between bites.

"Would you like to know what I'm going to do?" Jake asked Gillian. His arm was stretched out across the back of her chair, his fingers brushing her bare shoulder.

The band launched into its first song, and the other two couples at the table left for the dance floor.

"Are you doing something new?" Gillian asked Jake.

"Max doesn't need a cameraman anymore."

"What about the new guys?" Cara asked. It hadn't occurred to her that Jake would be out of a job.

"They can find their own cameramen. I've got things to do, places to go."

"What things?" Gillian seemed genuinely curious.

"I've been saving money for a while now," he told her.

"For?" she prompted.

"To start my own production company. Documentaries mostly, but maybe a little drama."

"Really?"

"Really."

While Cara watched the interplay, Max absently toyed with her diamond ring.

"It's nearly nine," he whispered in her ear.

"I'm not finished dessert yet," she whispered back.

"And what places?" Gillian's attention was fully on Jake.

"I'm looking for a good home base for the company." His fingers trailed along the tip of her shoulder. "I was thinking maybe Seattle."

"What a coincidence." Gillian smiled playfully, fluttering her fingers across the low cut of her dress. "*I* live in Seattle."

"What a coincidence," Jake echoed.

Cara leaned toward Max. "Should we give them some privacy?"

"We could go home," he suggested brightly.

"If you like, you could stay with me," Gillian offered.

Now Cara was more than a little curious.

"I could stay with you," Jake agreed, eyes warm.

Gillian's smile grew even more mischievous. "I have a nice little apartment above my garage."

"I'm not staying above your garage."

"It's got a view of the ocean, a pool, a lovely rose garden."

"I'm not staying above your garage," Jake repeated with certainty.

Gillian pouted. "You have other plans?"

Jake touched his index finger to her chin. "I definitely have other plans."

Cara pushed back her chair, turning to Max. "Dance, sweetheart?"

He laughingly and swiftly came to his feet, offering her his arm as they took their exit from the table.

Cara allowed herself one quick glance back and saw Jake lean in to kiss Gillian.

She looked up at Max. "Do you think they're…"

"If they're not," he answered, spinning her onto the floor and pulling her smoothly into his arms, "they're about to."

Cara easily matched her steps to Max's, smiling at the sight of her new ring.

"Thank you," she told him. "It's absolutely beautiful."

"I'm sorry I didn't have it when I proposed." He kissed her ring finger one more time.

"I got the feeling that was spontaneous," she told him.

"It was. Once I realized what a buffoon I'd been, I couldn't wait a second longer to make it better."

"I'm glad you didn't wait." Cara wouldn't have given up a moment of the past three days.

"I'm done with waiting. I want to be your husband as soon

as humanly possible." He paused. "Unless, of course, you want a big, fancy wedding."

"Do you want a fancy wedding?"

"I'll marry you in the National Cathedral or at a drive-through in Vegas. Just so long as you become my wife."

"No to the drive-through," she told him with a laugh.

"The National Cathedral?"

"Why don't we let Scarlet decide? She's the expert."

"Can we ask her to hurry?"

"Absolutely. Your baby needs a daddy, the sooner the better."

Max's hand gently cradled her stomach, intense, unvarnished love in his tone. "I'm going to try my best, Cara. I promise you. I'll read books. I'll take classes."

"You don't need classes," she told him, struggling not to tear up. "You're going to be a great father, Max. All you have to do is love our baby."

He gathered her close, a catch in his own voice. "Then it's going to be easy. Because I already do."

* * * * *

REQUEST YOUR FREE BOOKS!

2 FREE NOVELS PLUS 2 FREE GIFTS!

HARLEQUIN®

Desire

ALWAYS POWERFUL, PASSIONATE AND PROVOCATIVE

YES! Please send me 2 FREE Harlequin Desire® novels and my 2 FREE gifts (gifts are worth about $10). After receiving them, if I don't wish to receive any more books, I can return the shipping statement marked "cancel." If I don't cancel, I will receive 6 brand-new novels every month and be billed just $4.30 per book in the U.S. or $4.99 per book in Canada. That's a savings of at least 14% off the cover price! It's quite a bargain! Shipping and handling is just 50¢ per book in the U.S. and 75¢ per book in Canada.* I understand that accepting the 2 free books and gifts places me under no obligation to buy anything. I can always return a shipment and cancel at any time. Even if I never buy another book, the two free books and gifts are mine to keep forever.

225/326 HDN FVP7

Name _____ (PLEASE PRINT)

Address _____ Apt. #

City _____ State/Prov. _____ Zip/Postal Code

Signature (if under 18, a parent or guardian must sign)

Mail to the Harlequin® Reader Service:

IN U.S.A.: P.O. Box 1867, Buffalo, NY 14240-1867
IN CANADA: P.O. Box 609, Fort Erie, Ontario L2A 5X3

Want to try two free books from another line?
Call 1-800-873-8635 or visit www.ReaderService.com.

* Terms and prices subject to change without notice. Prices do not include applicable taxes. Sales tax applicable in N.Y. Canadian residents will be charged applicable taxes. Offer not valid in Quebec. This offer is limited to one order per household. Not valid for current subscribers to Harlequin Desire books. All orders subject to credit approval. Credit or debit balances in a customer's account(s) may be offset by any other outstanding balance owed by or to the customer. Please allow 4 to 6 weeks for delivery. Offer available while quantities last.

Your Privacy—The Harlequin® Reader Service is committed to protecting your privacy. Our Privacy Policy is available online at www.ReaderService.com or upon request from the Harlequin Reader Service.

We make a portion of our mailing list available to reputable third parties that offer products we believe may interest you. If you prefer that we not exchange your name with third parties, or if you wish to clarify or modify your communication preferences, please visit us at www.ReaderService.com/consumerschoice or write to us at Harlequin Reader Service Preference Service, P.O. Box 9062, Buffalo, NY 14269. Include your complete name and address.

SPECIAL EXCERPT FROM HARLEQUIN® KISS™

Evangeline is surprised when her past lover turns out to be her fiancé's brother. How will she manage the one she loved and the one she has made a deal with?

Follow her path to love January 22, 2013, with

THE ONE THAT GOT AWAY

by Kelly Hunter

"The trouble with memories like ours," he said roughly, "is that you think you've buried them, dealt with them, right up until they reach up and rip out your throat."

Some memories were like that. But not all. Sometimes memories could be finessed into something slightly more palatable.

"Maybe we could try replacing the bad with something a little less intense," she suggested tentatively. "You could try treating me as your future sister-in-law. We could do polite and civil. We could come to like it that way."

"Watching you hang off my brother's arm doesn't make me feel civilized, Evangeline. It makes me want to break things."

Ah.

"Call off the engagement." He wasn't looking at her. And it wasn't a request. "Turn this mess around."

"We need Max's trust fund money."

"I'll cover Max for the money. I'll buy you out."

"What?" Anger slid through her, hot and biting. She could feel her composure slipping away but there was nothing else for it. Not in the face of the hot mess that was Logan. "No," she said as steadily as she could. "No one's buying me out of anything, least of all MEP. That company is *mine,* just as much as it is Max's. I've put six years into it, eighty-hour weeks of blood, sweat, tears and fears into making it the success it is. Prepping it for bigger opportunities, and one of those opportunities is just around the corner. Why on earth would I let you buy me out?"

He meant to use his big body to intimidate her. Closer, and closer still, until the jacket of his suit brushed the silk of her dress, but he didn't touch her, just let the heat build. His lips had that hard sensual curve about them that had haunted her dreams for years. She couldn't stop staring at them.

She needed to stop staring at them.

"You can't be in my life, Lena. Not even on the periphery. I discovered that the hard way ten years ago. So either you leave willingly…or I make you leave."

Find out what Evangeline decides to do by picking up THE ONE THAT GOT AWAY by Kelly Hunter. Available January 22, 2013, wherever Harlequin books are sold.